First and foremos...
Best friends.

Kendrick didn't want to risk damaging that relationship. Not just because they worked together, but also because she meant a great deal to him. If necessary, he would gladly be just friends forever.

He thought of that one kiss they had shared. A smile tugged at his lips. It had actually been a part of the mission they were working together at the time. But he'd felt the connection as real as breathing. Good God, how he'd felt the connection. He'd been really careful since then. If a move happened between them, it would be because she initiated the action.

Jamie was the real deal, with an amazing family that he respected so much. She'd invited him to family celebrations on a number of occasions, and it was during their shared downtime that he really felt the pull. Whatever happened, he was giving her plenty of space and plenty of time to make a move.

The sound of footfalls on the stairs told him she was coming up to the second floor. He moved soundlessly to the door and leaned against it. She hesitated outside his door, and his heart bumped hard in his chest. Three seconds, then five elapsed before she went on into her room and closed the door. She'd wanted to say something or...

Give it a rest, Kenny.

Whatever she'd pondered during that brief pause, her sense of professionalism had prevented her from saying or doing whatever had crossed her mind.

For the best. For sure. This wasn't the time to get personal.

Dear Reader,

Nearly a quarter of a century ago, I submitted a story to Harlequin Intrigue. It was called *Safe by His Side* and it was the first story in a new series idea I called the Colby Agency. Some of my writer friends said I shouldn't submit a series idea since I was an unpublished newbie but I did it anyway. I've always had a habit of doing things my own way. And good thing, too. To date, sixty-two books in the Colby Agency have been published, and I have received so many fan letters. Victoria Colby became one of the most beloved characters of my writing journey.

It's been a while since I visited Victoria, and her grandchildren are all grown up now. But time hasn't stopped this power couple. She and Lucas are still providing the most discreet private investigations. I realized it was time to put Victoria and her family back on the page. Look for many new Colby Agency: The Next Generation stories to come. Don't worry, Victoria, Lucas and the other characters you've come to love are still there. If you're new to the Colby Agency, you'll love these stories, as well. Each one is a stand-alone journey, so no need to play catch-up. Don't miss a single one!

Best,

Debra

A COLBY CHRISTMAS RESCUE

USA TODAY BESTSELLING AUTHOR
DEBRA WEBB

Harlequin
INTRIGUE

Harlequin®
INTRIGUE™

ISBN-13: 978-1-335-45703-5

A Colby Christmas Rescue

Copyright © 2024 by Debra Webb

Harlequin Enterprises ULC
22 Adelaide St. West, 41st Floor
Toronto, Ontario M5H 4E3, Canada
www.Harlequin.com

Printed in Lithuania

MIX
Paper | Supporting responsible forestry
FSC® C021394

Debra Webb is the award-winning, *USA TODAY* bestselling author of more than one hundred novels, including those in reader-favorite series Faces of Evil, the Colby Agency and Shades of Death. With more than four million books sold in numerous languages and countries, Debra has a love of storytelling that goes back to her childhood on a farm in Alabama. Visit Debra at debrawebb.com.

Visit the Author Profile page at Harlequin.com.

CAST OF CHARACTERS

Victoria Colby-Camp—The head of the Colby Agency. Victoria never backs down from danger... but her weakness is her grandchildren. She will do anything to keep them safe.

Jamie Colby—Victoria's only granddaughter. Even at twenty-five, Jamie has made a name for herself in the world of spies and danger. But this will be her biggest test of all.

Kendrick "Kenny" Poe—An agent from the International Operations Agency—the first global initiative of its kind. Kenny drops everything to help Jamie.

Abidan "Abi" Amar—He is a private contractor with more secrets than the NSA. Can Jamie and Poe trust this man to help save her brother?

Luke Colby—The youngest member of the Colby family. When Luke is kidnapped, the whole family must do whatever necessary to rescue one of their own.

Lucas Camp—He and Victoria began as friends before she was married to James Colby, Lucas's best friend. But after James's death, Lucas spent the rest of his life keeping Victoria safe. When she agreed to be his wife, it was the best day of his life.

Dr. Quinton Case—He has perfected a neurosurgery technique that can save lives...but can he protect the lives of his own family?

Friday, December 21

Four Days Before Christmas

Chapter One

Victoria Colby stood at the window in her office that looked out over the street. This was one of her favorite places in the world and certainly she had traveled broadly. But here, in the Colby Agency offices, this window was her happy place. Watching the snow fall so close to Christmas was just icing on the cake. The winter storm had started two days ago, and the snow hadn't let up since. But, as Lucas reminded her, the storm wouldn't get in the way of their plans this year, so why not celebrate the deepening blanket of white?

It was the season after all.

Her heart felt heavy at the idea of not spending the holidays with her family. It was tradition. But that was impossible this year. Of course, she was literally surrounded by her agency family. Victoria and Lucas couldn't deny having an amazing extended family here at the agency.

And as wonderful as that was, it wasn't really the same.

The whole truth was that celebrating would be a lot more enjoyable if, for one, she didn't feel like her family were scattered so far and wide this holiday. And, secondly, she was worried sick about Tasha, her son Jim's wife. Jim and

Tasha were in Sweden and not for a vacation either. Tasha had been diagnosed with a rare type of cancer. Fortunately, Victoria had been able to get her into a cutting-edge research study that was showing very promising results with its participants. Victoria desperately needed this treatment to work. The idea of her son losing his wife—her precious grandchildren losing their mother—was simply unthinkable.

More unnerving at present: the children hadn't been told about the diagnosis. Tasha and Jim wanted to wait and see how things would go before telling their daughter and son. No point ruining their holidays as well, Jim had insisted. Victoria sighed, her heart heavier still. It wasn't like her grandbabies were actually children. Jamie was twenty-five now. Victoria still couldn't believe her granddaughter was so grown-up. She smiled and traced a melting flake of snow down the glass. Jamie had done everything early. Graduated high school and university years before her peers. Every three-letter government agency on the planet had sought her out well before she had that degree in her hand.

But Jamie had done what Jamie always did—exactly what *she* wanted to do. She had accepted an invitation to be one of only twelve Americans with the brand new International Operations Agency—or the IOA. Practically no one had a handle on exactly what this new multi-country agency was really, but the promise of great things was certainly being bragged about in all the highest places. This agency would extend far and wide, interweaving many allies together in a way never done before.

Victoria was extremely proud of Jamie for choosing a route with global implications, though she had to admit she would have preferred to have Jamie coming on board with the family business. The Colby Agency represented Victoria's life's work. She worried that after Jim there would be no one in the family to carry on the important work they did here.

Her grandson Luke, on the other hand, was just preparing to enter the last semester of his final year at university in Nashville, Tennessee. He was far less in a hurry to get on with his life. Another smile tugged at Victoria's lips. As a child, he had been so like his father. Extremely curious but not quite ready to jump in with both feet. He'd changed his major twice in his freshman year, before finally deciding to go into medicine and transferring to premed at Vanderbilt.

Victoria couldn't wait to see him spread his wings and come into his own.

With all that was going on in their lives, the kids wouldn't be coming home for Christmas either. Everyone—the world it seemed—was too busy. This made her far sadder than perhaps it should have, but this would be the first year that no one in the family had stayed in or come to Chicago to celebrate.

Lucas appeared behind her, and Victoria turned to him. "I fear it's going to be a lonely Christmas."

He touched her cheek with the backs of his fingers. "It's never lonely as long as we are together," he reminded her. "We're alive and well. We'll have plenty to celebrate."

Of course, he was right. She leaned into his strength, and they watched the snowflakes swirl and fall. Whether the family was here or not, it was going to be a beautiful few days. All of Chicago lay under a blanket of perfect, white snow giving the busy and at times troubled city such a peaceful appearance. How could anyone who loved this city not feel the magic of the season? At their ages it was important to enjoy each day all the more.

Victoria should be grateful, and she was. Who could blame her for missing her family?

"Slade mentioned," Lucas said, "that he and Maggie

planned to drop by after dinner at her mother's house. It will be nice to see them and to spend some time with Cody."

Another grandchild who was growing up so very fast.

"That would be lovely." Maggie's mother had no one else and Victoria certainly wouldn't selfishly resent the woman for having at least some family for the holiday even if it meant that Victoria and Lucas were alone. She and Lucas were so very lucky to still have each other.

The reminder that they would indeed have some family dropping by for the holidays brightened her spirits. Although they had not known about Slade until he was a grown man, he was as much a member of this family as anyone else. He had been raised by an evil woman who had done all in her power to turn him against Lucas, his biological father. But time and circumstances had changed that painful connection into a good, solid and loving relationship. One for which Victoria was immensely thankful. Lucas had sacrificed a great deal for his country. He deserved all the happiness that came his way.

"We should send everyone home after lunch," Victoria suggested. It was Friday after all, and the agency would be closed next week. All open cases had been closed by mid-December.

It was something they strove for each year beginning on the first of November. Having the last of the year's cases basically buttoned up by the holidays wasn't always possible, but they worked diligently toward that goal. There were some cases that simply couldn't be wrapped up so neatly in a certain time frame, but all efforts were made. This was good for her investigative team and for the clients they served.

Victoria had to admit that as careers went, she and Lucas had certainly enjoyed unusual ones. She, Lucas and James

Colby, her first husband, had begun their young lives together along with their careers working in the government. James and Lucas had been CIA—eventually leading a special black ops group like no other. In time, when Victoria and James had started a family, they had left the more dangerous work serving their government and started a private investigations agency.

But the past had not been ready to let them go and had drawn them deep into a whole other level of danger.

Victoria pushed the painful memories away. They had survived the nightmares and the tragedies and, thankfully, she and Lucas had found their way to each other in time. Although they had tried retirement and moving to a warmer climate, staying away from Chicago and the agency they had built was impossible.

"That is a very good idea, my dear." He kissed her cheek and then nuzzled it with his own. "Do you have something in mind for this evening?"

Victoria smiled. "I suppose we could be like the typical family and spend the weekend watching Christmas movies and baking cookies."

Lucas chuckled. "I don't think anyone would accuse us of being typical."

Victoria thought of the many, many cases they had investigated. The many times they had barely survived with their lives. "Oh yes, sometimes I forget that we're not like other couples."

During their nearly half-century-long careers, they had been kidnapped, shot at, had bombs left for them, had their entire office building burned down and, of course, one or both had been left for dead numerous times. Thankfully, they had always survived. At times by the sheer skin of their teeth.

Funny how even now, looking back at all those horrific situations, each one had been just another day at the office. And now, their granddaughter was following that same path with the IOA. Luke—not so much. Her grandson had chosen Vanderbilt University in Nashville for his premed work, where a great deal of amazing research was happening. And since Luke was a die-hard country music lover, Nashville was the perfect setting for him.

"I was thinking," Lucas said, "that we might consider a quick trip to Paris. I know how you love that city. A few days there would be a welcome change of pace. We'll be closer and available to rush to Sweden if Jim and Tasha need us. We can have the kids there in a matter of hours if need be."

Victoria held back her first response and mulled over the proposal. "You know, that's actually not a bad idea." Christmas in Paris. Yes. That would be very nice. "I'll run it by Ian and Simon to make sure they haven't made out-of-town plans already."

To her knowledge, none of the primaries at the agency were planning to travel out of town. She turned to her husband. "This was really a great idea, Lucas."

He smiled. "I already have reservations at the Shangri-La. I spoke to Jim yesterday and he was in agreement that he would prefer that we enjoy ourselves for the holidays and not wait around to hear news from Tasha's procedure."

So her husband and her son had been conspiring together. "Do you have flights already as well?" His smile widened to a grin. Why had she even asked? "This really is quite perfect, Lucas. Thank you."

Her cell vibrated against her desk. Victoria started for it and Lucas headed for the door. "I'll inform everyone that I told you about your Christmas present."

She should have known. "So everyone but me knew about this?"

"Not everyone." He grinned, then slipped out of her office.

Victoria shook her head. "Probably everyone but the janitor," she murmured with a laugh.

Luke flashed on the screen of her phone and Victoria's smile spread wider. "Luke," she said in greeting, "how wonderful to hear from you."

Her grandson was always busy, but even still he found a minute here and there to call his grandmother. He had probably heard about Lucas's surprise as well.

"Grandmother."

Victoria's smile faded. The clear and present fear she heard in her grandson's voice had her heart stumbling. "Luke, are you alright?" Had something happened to Tasha and Jim had already called the children? Dear God, she prayed that was not the case.

Had Luke been in an accident? He was speaking to her, which had to mean he was all right...wasn't he?

Or what if something had happened to Jamie?

A fresh wave of fear pounded in her veins.

"Listen to me very carefully, Grandmother," Luke said. "They're only allowing me a few moments to speak with you."

Victoria suddenly calmed. Inside, she went completely still and quiet while her instincts—the ones she had honed over nearly half a century—elevated to the highest state of alert. "I'm listening."

"They want ten million dollars. You have forty-eight hours. But you are not to do anything at all until you receive additional instructions." A pause. "I love you, Grandmother."

The call ended.

"Luke!" Victoria's heart burst into a frantic staccato. "Luke!" She stared at the black screen.

Victoria rushed from her office and paused in the private waiting room just outside the door. She immediately thought of Mildred, her dear assistant of so many years. How she wished she were here now.

Her new assistant gazed up at Victoria with a kind smile. "Is everything all right?"

"Rhea, I need Lucas, Nicole, Ian and Simon in my office *now*."

Rhea was fairly new, but she recognized there was trouble. Rather than bother with her phone, she ran from the room to personally gather everyone.

Needing to leave her own cell phone free, Victoria reached for the phone on Rhea's desk and called Chelsea Grant. Chelsea was their very best at tracing cell phone calls. "I need you in my office. Now please."

Five minutes later, those closest to Victoria were assembled in her office and she had provided the details of the call from Luke. She struggled to maintain her composure. Memories from when Jim had gone missing at age seven ripped at her insides. *This is not the same. Not the same.*

"The call came from the Nashville area," Chelsea confirmed. "But I'm having a difficult time narrowing down an exact location. The call bounced all over the Volunteer State like a football in a final play free-for-all. If another call originates from that phone, it's possible a drop in signal strength could create a hesitation in the smoke screen they're using. All I need is a call using that phone which lasts a few minutes and a couple of strength hesitations. The signal will automatically go to where it's strongest— where it originates."

"Thank you, Chelsea." Victoria turned to the others. "Thoughts?"

Ian Michaels and Simon Ruhl had been with Victoria

the longest of all her outstanding investigators. Nicole Reed Michaels, Ian's wife, was another of her most trusted. Between the three of them they had a world of experience and knowledge. More important, they were highly skilled in the art of evading danger and recovering assets.

"I'm hearing nothing from Interpol or our friend in the Mossad," Ian said. "My impression so far is that we're dealing with a domestic situation."

"I agree," Nicole confirmed. "My contacts in the CIA, the State Department and the NSA have heard no recent chatter related to our agency or anyone close to it."

Victoria wanted to be relieved at least a little, but she was not. She turned to Lucas. "What are you hearing from Thomas Casey?"

Like Lucas, Thomas Casey had once been a ghost of the highest order. A man who knew all things and who could go in and out of all places—wherever in the world—like smoke undetected. Their contacts and assets were scattered far and wide. But with that level of reach came fierce enemies…fierce competition.

"Ian and Nicole are correct," Lucas said, "this is not an international situation. This is someone closer to home."

"My contacts in the FBI—" Simon went next "—have confirmed rumblings in the southeast but nothing necessarily high level. Yet, they are not willing to take a bigger connection off the table."

Nicole rolled her eyes. "That's just like the Bureau. Always trying to make a situation bigger than it might be."

Simon shrugged. "They have agreed to put out feelers at the university and in the neighborhood where Luke lives."

"In my opinion," Ian said, "we should be heading in that direction even now."

"Luke said I was not to do anything until I received further instructions." The worry and uncertainty had Victoria's heart pounding again. No matter how many times she had faced life and death, knowing that a member of her family was in danger tore her apart inside.

"We should at least call Jamie," Lucas offered. He paced from the conference table to where Victoria sat on the edge of her desk, his trademark limp more visible than usual. He too was worried. These sorts of situations were far harder to tolerate at their ages.

And yet, they would die before backing down. She hoped whoever was behind this understood who they were dealing with.

"I don't want to call her," Victoria said, "until we have something more to share. At this point we know basically nothing."

Lucas leaned against Victoria's desk, putting himself next to her. "You're right, of course, but I feel as if we're doing nothing at all to alleviate the situation."

"The only part that gives me any relief is that Luke sounded somewhat calm despite the fear I heard in his voice," Victoria offered. "His tone was not as frantic as it could have been." Whether the rationale should or not, it gave her some sense of peace.

Nicole looked up from her tablet. "I've moved the requested ten million to a separate account—the one we generally use for ransom demands."

"Very good." Victoria should have already thought of that herself. Perhaps turning seventy-one last year had slowed her cognitively more than she'd realized. No. That wasn't true. There was absolutely nothing wrong with her brain. This was a problem with her heart.

And she was terrified.

"Luke has numerous friends," Simon mentioned, scrolling through the notes on his phone. "I've cued up a list with contact details in the event we need to start tracking them down. His professors. His class schedule. We have everything we need to begin a thorough search for him." His gaze settled on Victoria. "Whenever you say the word."

Her instincts urged her to act, but…the grandmother in her feared not following the directions given.

"We know from our contact at Nashville Metro that his car is at his condo. It hasn't left his parking space," Lucas said.

All their vehicles were tagged with state-of-the-art tracking devices. But having Nashville Metro confirm as much was good news indeed. "Which suggests," Victoria pointed out, "that wherever he is, someone picked him up or that person is at his condo with him." The latter was not likely since they all had panic buttons in their private homes as well. She felt confident Luke would have found a way to trigger that alarm.

The Colbys had suffered more than their share of losses. They did not take chances.

And yet, this ransom situation had happened just the same. Victoria felt powerless.

His cell phone had been turned off and the battery removed as soon as the call had ended, limiting its use as a tracking device. Victoria suspected his phone had only been used to ensure Victoria understood they did indeed have Luke in custody.

Ian said, "Nashville Metro have reported nothing in the way of hostage situations. There have been no new kidnappings in the past seventy-two hours. This appears to be an isolated event."

Nicole looked to Victoria once more. "I've run the enemy list through the steps and found no new activities."

Over the course of the past half century, the Colby name had amassed a good many powerful enemies. The activities of those enemies were closely monitored at all times. It was a necessary evil in the world of high-level investigations. The trouble was that new enemies cropped up and old enemies found fresh ways to hide. It was a never-ending cycle of discovery and catch up.

"Then we wait," Victoria said. There simply was no other choice. Waiting was far more difficult than taking action, but it was, at times, necessary.

Victoria's cell chimed with an incoming call.

Her heart rushed into her throat.

Jim.

"Don't tell him anything," Lucas urged.

As difficult as that would prove, Jim was thousands of miles away and could do nothing about what was happening here. He certainly didn't need the additional stress.

"How is Tasha?" Victoria decided coming straight out with the question was the best way to prevent herself from blurting the truth. Worry twisted inside her, slicing like barbed wire.

"She came through the preparation for the procedure quite well. The doctors are very hopeful."

Her son's voice sounded strained and so very tired. "This is wonderful news," Victoria said, fighting the sting in her eyes. Jim did not deserve this—whatever the hell it was. He had been through enough. Far more than most people were aware. His body bore the scars from the physical torture he had suffered from the moment he went missing as a child. The mental scars had taken years to put behind him. They would never be forgotten, but he had built a wonderful life and Victoria wanted nothing to tear that sweet life apart.

He had paid far more than his share already.

"She'll rest today and then the procedure will go as

scheduled tomorrow. If it's successful, we should know by Monday."

This was far sooner than Victoria had expected. If this did not go their way...no, she couldn't think that way.

"Is there anything we can do, Jim?" Victoria offered. "We all have you and Tasha in our prayers, of course."

"That is much appreciated, but we are hanging in there. The staff here is working diligently to make our time as stress free as possible."

"I'm so glad." Thank God. *Thank you, God.*

"I should go and be with Tasha. Please let Luke and Jamie know we're doing fine."

"I will," Victoria promised. "Don't worry about anything here. We have everything under control."

"Thanks, Mom. Love you."

Victoria's chest tightened. "Love you." The call ended and for a bit she stared at the dark screen and struggled to hold back her emotions.

Lucas placed his hand over her free one. "You did what you needed to do."

She nodded. Lowered the phone and looked from one of her dedicated friends to the next. "Whatever else we do, we must—"

Her cell chimed again. She gasped as the name on the screen flashed.

Luke.

"Let it ring once more," Chelsea said.

The phone chimed again, and Victoria answered. "Luke?"

"Grandmother, you will receive a letter of instruction from a special courier in fifteen minutes," he explained. "You are to follow the instructions in this letter very carefully. They have explained the first part of the instructions and I am supposed to pass that part along to you now."

His voice gave the impression of calm, but there was no missing the hum of fear just beneath the surface. The sound of it tore at her soul.

"Whatever we need to do," Victoria said. "Just name it."

"Besides the ten million dollars, there is something he needs and there is only one person who can get it for him."

Him. The person behind this was a man. The information wasn't surprising and wouldn't narrow things down much, but it was something—a small piece of the bigger puzzle. "All right. I'm listening."

There was silence on the line.

"Luke?"

The sound of struggling echoed in Victoria's ear. She held her breath, fear tightening her throat like a snake coiled around it. "Luke, is everything all right?"

"Yes." His answer was strained. "I don't want to tell you but I..." A breath blasted across the line. "I have no choice."

"It's all right, Luke. Tell me what you need, and I will make it happen."

"They want Jamie. She is the only one they will allow to do this. If anyone else tries...they say they will...*kill* me."

Panic rushed into Victoria's chest. "Luke, I—"

"Wait for the courier, Grandmother."

The call ended.

Terror slammed into Victoria, making her jerk with its impact.

"I'm calling Jamie now," Lucas said. "As soon as I know where she is I will send the plane for her."

Dear God. Victoria held tightly to the phone no matter that the connection to Luke was lost, her eyes closing in horror. Now they wanted her other grandchild.

Chapter Two

Jamie Colby watched the guy dressed as Santa stroll down Hollywood Boulevard. It wasn't like there was much of anything open. Just a diner or a coffee shop here and there. A tourist trap or three selling tickets for bus tours to the homes of the stars and other popular sites.

Jamie climbed out of her rented car and stepped to the sidewalk. "Santa has a new follower at three o'clock," she murmured for the microphone disguised as a necklace draped around her throat.

The guy in jeans and a torn T carrying a sign begging for donations had pushed away from the storefront he'd been holding up for about an hour and strolled after Santa. Both looked a little worse for the wear, like they'd slept in their clothes for a few days or a week. Not exactly a top-of-the-line Santa. More a low-rent version. *Who wants their kids sitting on the lap of a guy that sleazy looking?*

But Jamie wasn't complaining. Working an op in LA around Christmas was way better than rambling around her apartment in DC. It was cold and wet in DC. Today in LA—Hollywood actually—it was a pleasant sixty-eight degrees with the sun shining. In a couple more hours the streets would be filled with tourists and life would be buzzing like bees in a honeycomb.

She liked the sunshine and the life beat of this place.

The only downside in her opinion was that after an entire month of hanging around the LA area, Jamie still hadn't stumbled upon any big celebrities. A few unknowns and lots and lots of wannabes. The city was always awash with people who wanted to possess just a little bit of the magic that came from Hollywood. The problem was most would never know what it was like to be a celebrity. Most would work in the service industry or something not exactly legal until they disappeared into obscurity or went back home to Kansas or wherever with their tails tucked between their legs. It was not a journey for the faint of heart.

Jamie had to admit that she'd had the dream once—at fourteen. She'd been in love with the idea of a career on the big screen. What young girl hadn't flirted with the idea? But her grandmother had known exactly how to change her mind. She brought Jamie for a weeklong stay in LA. They'd seen the sights and they'd also seen the parts that no one wanted to talk about—Victoria Colby had made sure of the latter. The reality of life in a big city that was really like a nation of its own with all the issues and ups and downs that went along with a huge population was not such a fairy tale. Bottom line—not everyone could be a star.

Jamie smiled when she thought of her grandmother. Victoria had a way of clarifying all things. She missed her so much. It was snowing in Chicago right now. Jamie wished she was going home for Christmas, but she was on assignment here and her parents had taken a long overdue vacation to Europe. Luke was staying in Nashville to be a part of a special program between semesters. The guy was always looking for ways to gain extra credit. Jamie didn't get it. Anything beyond a 4.0 GPA was totally unnecessary in her view. But good grades had always come easy for her. Luke had to work for his.

"Heads up, Colby."

The words whispered in her earpiece brought her back to full attention. Santa was still making his way along the sidewalk, crossing over Vine. The errant beggar had gained on him to the point of nearly overtaking him.

"It's going down soon," came the voice in her ear.

Jamie picked up her pace and made an agreeable sound for those listening, including her partner.

Every move she made—every move her team made—was under close scrutiny. No one wanted this new agency to fail. But the powers that be weren't interested in throwing money after a new venture that on first look seemed too similar to the ones they already had. In truth there were already far too many government agencies—particularly secretive ones—in the opinion of some. For IOA to survive it had to provide something none of the others did and it had to be better…in every way.

Jamie wanted to be a part of making that happen. Like her grandmother, making a name for herself and a good career just wasn't enough. She wanted to make her special *mark*. A mark no one else had made.

Her friend Kendrick Poe would say she was overthinking it, but he'd already made one hell of a mark for himself so he should totally understand even if he pretended his accomplishments were no big deal.

Besides, just being a Colby set the bar damned high.

For a girl, Luke would say.

Jamie bit back a grin. Her little brother was certain he would go far higher than his big sister.

Not if Jamie could help it.

She was all for her brother going as far as possible as long as she went further. They'd been fiercely competitive—especially with each other—forever.

Up ahead, the beggar guy moved in a little closer on Santa.

Time to move.

Jamie added another click to her pace and walked past the beggar. He glanced at her, but considering her too-tight jeans and cropped sweater he didn't appear to consider her a threat.

Too bad for him.

She had just powered in front of Santa when she turned over her supercool right ankle boot and threw her full body weight into the guy in the red and mostly off-white velvet.

They both went down, landing uncomfortably on the concrete sidewalk.

Beggar guy stared in astonishment for one seemingly endless moment before hurrying away. He'd missed his shot. Too bad. Too sad.

"I'm so sorry!" Jamie cried as she attempted to right herself and Santa. "Are you all right, sir?"

He should be all right, but he smelled way wrong. Inside, she shuddered. Santa needed a serious shower and a freshly laundered suit. He smelled a little like sweat and a lot like alcohol. Jamie really hoped the stain on the front of his jolly jacket wasn't dried vomit.

The man scrambled for his red hat and tugged it back on before allowing Jamie to help him to his feet.

"I'm fine," he insisted, looking around exactly like a criminal would.

When would people learn? If you wanted to do a job well—even an illegal one—you had to get your act together and leave the booze at home.

"Oh no." Jamie dusted at his coat, noting how the right sleeve had come loose from the body of the jacket at the seam. "You tore your jacket. I hope you weren't on the way to a scheduled Santa visit."

"No." He shook his head, then backed away just enough to look her up and down. "You okay, little girl?"

She smiled and resisted the initial response that shot to the tip of her tongue. She was no little girl. The term was probably just the way he referred to all females younger than him, which would include most of the population in the LA area.

"I think I twisted my ankle." She winced. "I should have been paying better attention to where I was going."

"Probably on your phone," he grumbled, testing his own weight on first his left foot, then his right.

Apparently, he actually had twisted an ankle. Could make her job easier.

"I'm so sorry. Really." She offered her arm. "I insist on seeing you to your destination."

She noted the way he stared beyond her. "Beggar guy is coming back around," the voice whispered in her earpiece. No wonder Santa was staring.

When the collision had occurred the other guy apparently crossed the street and now he was retracing his steps. He had a mission. Good for him. Too bad he'd failed already.

"Well…er…" Santa nodded. "I could use the help."

He was old enough, maybe even close to her grandmother's age. No one would be surprised at him asking for help after a spill at his age. Beggar guy would just have to back off for a bit.

"How long have you been playing Santa?" Jamie asked

as they walked slowly forward. She purposely set the pace
slow to buy time and to wear on beggar guy's patience.

"Off and on since I hit sixty-five. The cost of living in
LA is difficult on a fixed income."

"I'm sure." LA living wasn't easy on a great income.
"So, you're a lifer?"

"Born and raised," he said with a glance over his shoulder.

She chuckled. "I'm surprised you're not an actor or a
former one." He actually looked like the type.

"Who says I'm not." He glanced at her this time. "Never
judge a book by its cover, little girl."

How ironic. She'd just been thinking the same thing.

"We have a newcomer to the party."

The warning echoed in her earpiece. Time to wrap up
the chitchat.

Jamie reached to her left hip pocket as if she were reach-
ing for her cell and slipped out the lightweight handcuffs.
She'd slapped the first cuff on Santa's wrist before he realized what she was doing. Simultaneously, she tugged him
toward the No Parking sign and snapped the other cuff to
the metal post.

Then she whirled and confronted beggar guy who had
stopped to stare in shock at what she'd done.

Didn't see that one coming, did you?

There were a few pedestrians on the street. No one
wanted to whip out a gun. Well, at least not Jamie. She
hoped to do this the old-fashioned way by kicking beggar
guy's butt. And then he reached into his jacket and came
out with a weapon.

Damn it.

She kicked the beggar's gun out of his hand before he
had it fully leveled on her. Santa was shouting and attempting to tug himself free. *Good luck with that.*

"The newcomer is coming at you," she heard from her earpiece.

"Great," she muttered as beggar guy dove at her. She rolled him into a hold with one arm locked around his throat and her legs locked around his, prying them apart to prevent him from gaining purchase on the ground. Good thing her tight jeans were made of spandex. When he continued to resist, she pounded his head into the concrete a couple of times, and he relaxed.

Newcomer was suddenly on top of her then.

This one was dressed like Batman and wasn't going down quite so easily.

He flipped Jamie onto her back and had both hands around her throat. She clawed at his face. Before she could get in a good dig, his head suddenly jerked to the right and then his body flew off her.

"I thought you might need a hand." A long-fingered hand reached out to her.

She looked from the hand she recognized to the guy in the Wolverine costume.

Poe.

"Really? Wolverine?" Jamie took his hand and allowed him to pull her to her feet. "I had this, you know."

"I'm sure you did," Poe agreed, "but Santa was causing a scene and we don't need that."

The old guy was shouting at the top of his lungs and people were stopping to stare and point. Cell phones were coming out.

Time to go.

"Where's the car?" she asked as she freed Santa.

"Half a block up on the right."

"Let's go, Santa." She secured the newly freed cuff to

her wrist. She wasn't letting this guy out of her sight and certainly not out of her reach.

By the time she ushered him forward that half a block or so, Poe had hopped behind the wheel. Jamie opened the rear passenger door and she and Santa climbed into the back seat.

"What's going on here?" Santa demanded.

When Poe had peeled away from the curb, she glanced back to ensure the two followers were still dragging themselves off the ground.

"Not to worry, Santa," she assured him. "We're not sending you back to the North Pole yet."

"Am I under arrest?" Santa demanded. "I need to see a badge. And aren't you supposed to read me my rights?"

"What's wrong with Wolverine?" Poe demanded from the front seat as he took a right on Sunset Boulevard.

Jamie checked behind them to ensure they weren't being followed. "I had you figured for a Deadpool guy."

"Where are we going?" Santa demanded.

"Don't worry," Jamie assured him. "We're going to take very good care of you, Santa."

Poe took Sunset all the way to where it transitioned into West Cesar Estrada Chavez Avenue and then a left on North Main to Our Lady Queen of Angels Catholic Church. This was the drop point. If they were lucky, they would get in and get out without a confrontation.

No one wanted to cause turmoil in a house of God just days before Christmas.

They parked across the street and surveyed the area.

"If they're in the church already…" Poe said without completing the thought.

Jamie understood. If the others were in the church already, they were in trouble. In truth, they had no way of confirming how many of the *others* were on this.

"Let's assume we got here first," Jamie offered.

"Whatever you say." Her partner wasn't so optimistic.

Poe got out and leaned against the closed driver's side door to keep an eye on their destination.

While he got the lay of the land, Jamie needed to convince Santa to cooperate. "Look, I don't know why you needed an exit strategy today, Santa," she began, "but I would prefer to keep breathing so don't give me any trouble. Got it?"

His face wrinkled with confusion. "What in God's name is an exit strategy?"

Clearly the man had not watched enough James Bond. "Someone wants you dead and we're here to make sure that doesn't happen. We extracted you before you reached the location where you were supposed to die, on the corner of Hollywood Boulevard and McFadden Place."

"I was meeting my nephew for lunch."

"I'm sorry to tell you this, but your nephew or someone close to him set you up." She unlocked the handcuffs and tossed them onto the floorboard. "I need you to stay close to me, Santa."

He nodded, the movement unsteady as if the news had knocked him for a loop. Probably had.

The rear driver's side door opened. "We seem to be clear to proceed," Poe said.

Which meant he actually couldn't be certain. Evidently the communication link had dropped. The voices in Jamie's ear had disappeared.

They were on their own without the assist of handy electronics.

Santa eased out and Poe stepped closer, shielding the older man's body with his own.

Jamie emerged on the opposite side and surveyed the sidewalk and the strip mall beyond it on the passenger side, then she crossed around to the other side of the car with Poe and their Christmas package.

"Going in the front door." Poe glanced at her.

Jamie nodded.

They hurried across the street and to the double entry front doors of the church, Santa in tow between them.

The doors were locked.

What the hell?

"Side door," Jamie urged.

They moved around the front right corner of the church, going for the side entrance. Their destination was the door beneath the portico that allowed for dropping off parishioners under the cover of an awning. All they had to do was reach it before they encountered trouble.

Jamie kept a close watch on their surroundings. No one behind them.

No one in front.

No running or shouting.

So far, so good.

Her pulse kept a rapid staccato while they hustled along the side of the building until they reached the secondary entrance. They entered without hesitation.

Inside was dark.

The side door opened into a quiet corridor. Taking a left led to the main sanctuary. Right went toward restrooms and a family room for breastfeeding mothers. Jamie had studied the layout.

"Why are we here?" Santa asked in a too-loud whisper.

"You'll be picked up here," Jamie assured him. At least as long as things went according to plan. She kept that part to herself. No need to get the guy riled up again.

Santa stalled, tugging to free his arm from her grip. "I don't understand."

This was not the time. "As soon as we ensure your pickup detail is here, I'll explain as best I can."

The sound of the door they had entered only moments ago opening had Jamie and Poe parting ways. He went toward the main sanctuary, while she ushered Santa into a coat closet near the restrooms.

The coat closet was actually a room with plenty of hanging space for coats, shelves for hats and hooks for umbrellas. It had once been the only restroom and had housed several stalls, so it was fairly large for the purpose it now served.

"I think there must have been a mistake," Santa whispered.

Jamie pressed a hand to his mouth in hopes of getting the message across without having to say the words out loud.

Under her sweater, in the band that kept her cell pressed against her abdomen, her cell vibrated with an incoming call. Control, the people in charge of this operation, would not contact her via her private cell phone. If the comms link was down, someone would contact her or Poe in person.

The call was more likely a distraction.

She hated the idea that someone might have gotten her private cell number, but it happened. If that proved to be the case, she'd need a new number after this. Always a pain in the butt.

Footsteps in the corridor outside the coat closet had her bracing. She scanned the room and then ushered Santa into the farthest corner from the door. She grabbed the two big coats that someone had left behind and camouflaged him as best she could.

She was about to leave it at that when she noticed the open lid on the built-in wood bench that ran the length of the wall. She tapped Santa on the shoulder and pointed to the big bench. It was at least two feet from front to back. Slightly taller than that and several feet long.

He shrugged and then climbed in. Jamie poked all signs of red velvet into the bench and closed the lid. She placed an umbrella atop it and quickly moved toward the door. She flattened against the wall next to it.

Perfect timing. The door opened. She stepped back, keeping the door between her and whoever was coming in.

As soon as the door started to close, and she spotted the back of the head now swiveling on a pair of broad shoulders, she knew it was not a friend. Definitely a foe.

She reached up, boring the muzzle of her weapon into the back of his skull. "Stop right there."

Surprisingly, he did as she asked.

"Put your weapon on the floor and kick it aside," she ordered.

Rather than bend over to do as she asked, he did what she would have done, he began to lower in the knees.

Oh well, if that was the way he wanted to play it.

Just when he would have twisted to put one between her eyes, she squeezed her own trigger, sending a bullet into his right wrist and sending the weapon he'd been holding flying toward the floor.

He swore. Grabbed for her.

She pressed the muzzle between his eyes. "Don't make me shoot you again. I won't be so nice about it this time."

He glared at her, but his hands went up, blood running down from the right wrist.

The door flew inward again, but this time it was Poe.

"Well, hello," he said to the guy with the bullet wound. "I see you met my partner."

Five minutes later, their pickup crew had arrived, and Santa was on his way to safety.

Jamie had no idea why the man had needed assistance or even who he was. She had no need to know, any more than Poe did. Their mission was to provide him with an exit strategy from his planned engagement and to get him to this church.

They might never know what value he represented, but they had accomplished their mission and that was all that mattered.

Once they were in the rented car, headed away from Our Lady Queen of Angels, Poe said, "You hungry? I'm starving."

Completing a mission was a big rush and it always left her hungry. "How about we get out of LA before we stop."

He hitched his head in acknowledgment. "How about we drive down to the Santa Monica Pier and find something to eat and listen to the ocean roar."

"Somewhere in Malibu will be quieter," she argued. "Too many tourists on the pier."

"Works for me."

Like her, her partner wore jeans and a pullover. His was a UCLA sweatshirt. He was a year older than Jamie and had darker features—brown hair, brown eyes—that sharply contrasted her blond hair. They had been friends for almost two years now. He was a good friend. They teetered on the edge of something more, but work always got in the way. Probably for the best. Who had time for romance?

Her cell started vibrating again, and Jamie reached beneath her sweatshirt and pulled it free of its hiding place.

G flashed on her screen.

She smiled. Her grandmother. "Hey, Grandmother," she said. "Is it still snowing in Chicago?"

"Jamie, we have a problem."

Fear trickled into her blood. "What kind of problem?"

"It's Luke. Someone has taken him, and he needs our help." Victoria's voice trembled on the last word.

There were things she should say. Like how terrible it was to hear this news and why would anyone target Luke? But her throat had closed, and she couldn't seem to make her jaw work.

"Jamie." The male voice she knew as well as her own underscored just how serious the situation was. If her grandmother was so upset…

No jumping to conclusions. Her heart stuttered again, and she managed a breath. She had to listen carefully. "Yes, Grandpa." She swallowed at the lingering tightness in her throat. "What's going on?" Calling Lucas Camp "Grandpa" was like calling a grizzly bear a kitten.

"Colby One will pick you up at the Van Nuys Airport at one. We'll meet you in Nashville."

Poe was splitting his attention between her and the road. He couldn't hear the conversation, but he obviously saw the terror on her face. "What's going on?" he urged.

Jamie made a decision then and there. They had completed their mission. Time off was a given. It was only a matter of how much. "Inform the pilot I'm bringing a friend. I'll see you in Nashville, Grandpa."

She ended the call, and Poe's gaze locked with hers. She explained the situation, the need to scream crawling up her throat. She had to stay calm. Focused. "We have to find him. I…can't…" Big breath. "I can't let him down."

"Don't worry," Poe said softly. "We won't fail… We never have before."

He was right…but this time was different. This was not just another mission… This was her little brother.

Chapter Three

The private airfield near Nashville was off the beaten path, but then Jamie suspected that was why it had been chosen. Whether it was the fear that their calls were being monitored or could potentially be so, there had been radio silence during the four-plus-hour flight from LA to Nashville. She'd contacted their superior at IOA and notified him that she and Poe would be out of reach for a few days. Since they were due time off after an operation it was no problem.

Poe had helped Jamie keep herself together. Not an easy task when she was worried. Luke was not like her. He hadn't embraced this undercover, secret agent life. He was a total pacifist—a man focused on learning how to help others with medicine. Although Victoria had insisted they both learn how to use a handgun, Jamie would bet Luke had not touched one since.

"That's your grandmother?" Poe asked as he watched Victoria emerge from the limo that had arrived.

Jamie smiled. She tried to think how Victoria Colby-Camp appeared to others. A mature woman with silver threads in her dark hair. Tall, trim, well dressed. She looked a good twenty years younger than her age. From all appearances she might be your average attractive, wealthy middle-aged woman.

Except there was nothing average about Victoria.

"That's her." They had used a different airfield. Having two jets arrive from Chicago at the same place would have roused suspicions. Jamie rushed to her grandmother and hugged her as hard as she dared. Even so, she was impressed at the slim, toned body she felt beneath the layers of clothing. Victoria not only kept her mind sharp, but she also kept her body lean as well.

"Jamie." Victoria drew back and looked her up and down. "We don't have a lot of time, so we need to talk fast."

Renewed worry twisted in Jamie's belly. "What can you tell me?"

"Let's talk inside."

Jamie turned to her grandpa, who was watching them across the top of the vehicle. She smiled. "Hey, Grandpa." She hitched her head toward the man waiting behind her. "This is Poe. We work together."

Lucas Camp pointed a gaze at Poe that likely sent a shiver down his spine.

"Sir." Poe gave him a nod.

"Poe," Jamie said, drawing his attention in her direction, "this is my grandmother, Victoria."

Her mission partner nodded. "A pleasure to meet you, ma'am. I've heard a lot about you." He glanced toward Lucas. "Both of you."

Victoria nodded before ducking back into the passenger compartment of the limo. Jamie climbed in behind her. Lucas settled on the seat next to Victoria, and Poe dropped next to Jamie opposite her grandparents.

"What in the world happened?" Worry about her little

brother had torn Jamie apart during the flight here. She wasn't sure how much more of the not knowing she could handle.

"I received a call this morning," Victoria explained. "It was Luke. He said I would receive instructions via a courier and that I should do nothing until I received those instructions. The only thing he could tell me before hanging up was that it had to be you who carried out the instructions."

Jamie and Poe exchanged a look.

"Then, we can safely assume," Poe suggested, "that this someone is aware of your particular skill set."

Jamie nodded. "Agreed."

Lucas said, "We have some idea of what your work entails. What aspects of that work do you believe has put you in someone's crosshairs?"

Jamie thought about the question for a moment. "As you know," she explained, "our agency operates a very diverse team to resolve issues all over the world. Sometimes, like today, our assignments seem sedate."

"Like picking up a Santa-for-hire," Poe clarified, "before he was neutralized and delivering him to a safe location."

Jamie went on. "We have no idea who this Santa was or why someone wanted to terminate him. Frankly, it seemed like the sort of assignment any cop in the LAPD could have handled. But there was a reason we were sent in to do it. We just may never know what that reason was."

"I can shed a little light on that one," Lucas said.

Poe frowned and shared another look with Jamie.

"You have no idea," she said, laughing. "Grandpa isn't who you think he is." This was truer than she would ever be able to convince her friend or anyone else.

Poe gave a nod. "I see."

"Your Santa arrived in LA from a visit to Santiago last

Friday. His wife's mother passed away unexpectedly."
Lucas shrugged. "We'll stick with calling him Santa. You
may not realize based on his condition today—he has felt
a little under the weather the past couple of days—but he
was booked solid with many appearances at some very
large malls and department stores."

Jamie got it now. "He would have come into contact with
a lot of people over the next few days."

Lucas nodded. "By tomorrow, the incubation period will
be complete and Santa will be highly contagious with the
virus he contracted at the funeral."

"I take it he had no idea," Jamie suggested. No wonder
he'd been self-medicating with alcohol. He probably felt
like hell and was attempting to cheer himself up.

"None. Eleven other targets were discovered and picked
up in the past twenty-four hours. Your Santa was the last."

"Wow." Poe shook his head. "No wonder we had to take
all those shots when we received our orders."

"There's no reason to believe you were exposed," Lucas
explained. "The date and time your Santa was exposed was
known so he wouldn't have been contagious yet, just feeling a little under the weather from all the changes happening in his body."

Victoria shook her head. "I liked it better when we could
see the attacks coming." She took a deep breath. "At any
rate, based on the instructions delivered by the courier Luke
told us about, there is a certain surgeon in Nashville who
has perfected a previously basically impossible-to-do brain
surgery. The first successful procedure was completed just
three months ago. There have been two more each week
since and though this is an amazing step, this surgeon is
the only one so far who has managed the feat. The hope
is that he will be able to train others, but it's not going to

be easy, and worse, it's going to take time. For those who have inoperable brain tumors, time is not on their side."

"There is a great deal of fiery rhetoric in the medical field just now," Lucas said, picking up from there, "as to whether this surgeon, Dr. Quinton Case, should be wasting his time trying to teach others to do the surgery or just doing the surgery. He can only do two or three per week because it is incredibly tedious and both physically and mentally exhausting."

Victoria said, "How do you decide which patients will receive the surgery and which won't during any given week? How many lives will be lost while time is taken away from surgery to attempt teaching others?"

"Wow, that's a hard one." Jamie searched her grandmother's face. "But, as horrible as what you're telling me is, what does this have to do with Luke?"

"We can only assume that our kidnapper has someone close to him who needs this surgery since all he wants is the surgeon."

Jamie held up her hands. "Wait. This dude wants me to kidnap this surgeon and deliver him to his location of choice?"

"You have approximately seventy-two hours—or until five o'clock on Monday. At that time, if the surgeon has not been delivered to the drop-off location, Luke will die."

Jamie's heart sank. She turned to Poe. "Though I appreciate your desire to give me a hand with this, I think this is where your participation ends. I can't ask you to do this."

"No way." He shook his head. "I'm not walking away."

"I won't argue with you, Kenny." She wouldn't waste time or energy doing that.

"Then don't because I'm not leaving until you do." He leaned deeper into the seat.

"You should consider what she's trying to tell you," Lucas argued. "There is nothing we can do. In fact, this… right here…is as far as our participation can go. The instructions were explicit. Once we have passed the information along, any involvement on our part or the part of our agency will prompt an immediate termination of the deal. No exceptions."

Jamie turned to her grandfather. Then it was decided— she was on her own. "Under the circumstances, I would suggest you get on with this briefing and go."

Victoria shook her head. "There are steps we can take to prevent you having to do this."

Jamie understood. They could make a preemptive strike. Grab the surgeon and then do the negotiating. "But we both understand how risky that option is. The same with going to the FBI. Anything we do puts us in a situation where we can't guarantee the outcome for Luke."

Victoria shook her head again. "Even following their rules, there are no guarantees of the outcome, Jamie. As you're well aware, things can go wrong either way. People can go back on their word."

"Then there's nothing to talk about." Jamie looked to Lucas. "Let's get this done and the two of you should be on your way. It doesn't take a lot of imagination to figure out they likely know about your arrival, and they'll be watching for your departure."

Lucas passed Jamie a brown envelope. "This tells you everything you need to know about your target. The drop-off location will be given to you nearer the grab time."

Jamie accepted the package. "Thank you."

Lucas shook his head and looked away.

"The limo will drop you at the first transition point

where you'll receive the next set of instructions," Victoria said.

"As you said, they know we're here and we have been instructed," Lucas said, his voice tight, "to get back to Chicago."

"I'll take care of this." Jamie looked from her grandfather to her grandmother. "Luke will be fine. I promise." She hesitated a moment. "I'm assuming you haven't told my parents."

"We've been instructed not to tell anyone," Victoria confirmed.

Jamie reached out and took her grandmother's hand. "I will get this done."

They hugged and then Jamie hugged her grandfather. There were so many things she would have liked to say, and she was confident her grandparents felt the same, but there was no time.

Luke needed them to remain calm and to move quickly. All else would have to wait.

Excalibur Court,
6:30 p.m.

JAMIE HAD WAITED at the airfield until the Colby Agency jets had taken flight. Watching her grandparents leave knowing she had to stay and get this done had been extremely difficult. This was her little brother's life, and her grandparents were the strongest, most capable people she knew. She suddenly felt utterly lost and desolate.

The driver had then brought them to a house in a very high-end neighborhood. The house was apparently unoccupied and sat in a cul-de-sac on a hillside overlooking the home of Dr. Quinton Case. Well, calling the place a home was a bit of an understatement. The Case's estate was a massive property ensconced amid more than a hundred acres of treed serenity.

The house on Excalibur Court had been staged with everything they might need—at least on first look. The supersensitive telescope setup allowed them to see—to a degree—inside the home of Dr. Case. Everything from climbing equipment to serious weapons and one hell of a muscle car getaway vehicle had been provided.

There was food and drink, but Jamie wasn't consuming anything in this house. She'd had the driver stop at a local market where she'd picked up food and water. She and Poe had searched the house for wires and cameras. They'd found numerous devices, though they couldn't be sure they'd found them all.

Whoever had set up this op was good.

Strangely enough, a note for Jamie *and* Poe had been left on the kitchen island. The person who had composed the note claimed to have known she would bring Poe with her and the items he would need had been made available as well. This included clothes and weapons. To Jamie's way of thinking, this was proof whoever was behind this knew both her and Poe.

Poe had spread the map and step-by-step instructions on the dining table. Whoever was funding this op had thought of everything—literally.

"On Sunday night, Case is having a holiday party at his home," Poe said. "And that's when you're supposed to nab him."

"The presumption," Jamie said, "I assume is that this is a time when he will be most vulnerable. Preoccupied. Distracted."

The man was surrounded by security at all times, particularly at his office and at the hospital. Understandable, she supposed. But it was sad that because of his success in creating a lifesaving procedure his life was now in danger.

"No question," Poe agreed. "I'm thinking…" He leaned against the edge of the table. "I find it interesting that they assumed you would want me to come because there was nothing in the instructions about me and no one has showed up to put a bullet in my head or ask me to take a walk. Instead, they left clothes and weapons for me."

"Seems like they know me—us—pretty well," she agreed.

"Makes sense I guess since it doesn't seem like a one-person operation if you ask me," he pointed out.

"Since we haven't been given more detail other than the strike is on Sunday night, I'd say it's too soon to tell. But I tend to agree with you. I'm wondering if we'll be given additional backup when the time comes."

Jamie walked into the living room and up to the telescope. The wall of floor-to-ceiling glass doors opened fully to the balcony outside by sliding away like a movable wall. Not so great this time of year, but amazing for extending the entertaining space to the outdoors in the summer. She peered through the lens and directly into the entrance hall of the grand manor that was Dr. Case's home. "The real question in my mind is getting him out of those woods."

Poe joined her at the wall of windows that looked out over the dark landscape. "Getting him out of the house shouldn't be so difficult. There are numerous egresses. It will only be a matter of evading staff and security. The cameras will be another issue altogether, but they may be providing information on the security system. One would hope."

"It's the woods," she repeated as she surveyed the darkness between this house and the target. "He's not going to come willingly, and we have to be extremely careful with him. Any injury could put him out of commission. That would defeat the whole purpose of nabbing him."

"And therein," Poe said, "lies the answer to why we are here."

Jamie straightened away from the telescope, following his train of thought. "They need him for his ability to do this procedure."

"Which means," Poe picked up where she left off, "our employer either intends to start a school for surgeons who want to be like Case, or, as your grandmother suggested, he has a loved one with an inoperable brain tumor who doesn't have the time left to wait his or her turn for the procedure."

It wasn't necessary to say the rest out loud just in case they were being monitored. Even now, Victoria and her people would likely be running down known patients in need of the potentially lifesaving surgery only Dr. Case could provide. Even if they narrowed the list down to the precise patient and therefore the perpetrator of this plan, would there be time to find Luke wherever they had hidden him?

The risk was entirely too great to take.

The sound of clapping had them both spinning to face the threat. "Bravo."

Poe reached for his weapon.

Jamie was too busy picking her jaw up off the floor. Even if she hadn't seen his face, she would have recognized that hint of a British accent anywhere. "Abi?"

Abidan "Abi" Amar stood near the French doors that led to the living room. He clapped one last time before dropping his hands to his sides. "Jamie." One eyebrow reared up. "Kendrick Poe, I presume," he said to Poe. "A man whose claim to fame is that he purports to be a distant relative of Edgar Allan Poe. How very interesting."

"Actually—" Poe put his weapon away "—my claim to fame is the well-known exit of no less than a dozen Americans from al-Qaeda in Yemen. Everything else I've done in my short career is just icing on that very large cake."

Abi gave a nod. "I may have heard something about that."

"What're you doing here, Abi?" Jamie crossed her arms over her chest and eyed him suspiciously.

To say his appearance was a surprise would be a vast understatement. Abi was not a terrorist, though many might say his reputation suggested otherwise. Be that as it may, her knowledge of him provided some room for error in that assessment.

Abi was a contractor who worked doing whatever he was paid to do—within some vague lines that only he could see. In other words, he wasn't a real bad guy. Just one who did things that were not always legal for money.

He colored outside the lines and he loved every minute of it.

"It is my job to oversee your work," he announced. He surveyed Poe up and down. "Although, I must say my job may have been easier without this complication."

Poe's face darkened. "Excuse me?"

Jamie held up a hand for Poe as she walked toward Abi. "So, you're my backup in this?"

"That is correct."

"Wait a minute, Jamie," Poe argued.

Again, she gave Poe her hand. "First, Abi—" she looked directly at him "—I would not trust you to have my back under any circumstances. Ever. Second, if this…whoever-he-is…that took my brother has you, what does he need with me? I can't fathom why he would *complicate* this situation with additional players. More room for leaks and other issues."

The last was the real question. Abi's skills were equal to Jamie's, maybe greater since he was older and had more experience. He had been offered a position at IOA without even putting his name in the hat or competing in any way, but he'd turned it down. He much preferred being his own boss. He didn't play well with others.

If the person who took Luke—who wanted or needed Dr. Case—had Abi on the payroll, they really didn't need anyone else for a straightforward op like this. In fact, the scenario made no sense at all.

"You see," Abi said, "trust is a very important part of this very delicate situation. I think my reputation for being available to the highest bidder preceded me and the trust level wasn't where it needed to be."

"Good point," Jamie agreed. Abi was just as likely to abduct the doctor and sell his services to someone else as to go with the guy who hired him.

Abi went on, "This is also the reason, I suspect, that they took your brother. A little insurance to keep you focused."

Abi was very handsome by any standards. Tall, muscular, black hair and eyes. Jamie stood no more than three feet from Abi and already the physical draw wanted to overpower her. No way. She had been down that road once. Besides, she could only have one focus right now: rescuing her brother.

The very last thing she intended to do was get involved in any way with this man. He was dangerous on far too many levels.

"What do you know that we don't?" she demanded.

"Really? I'm not sure we have the time to cover everything."

Poe shook his head. "This guy is a real comedian."

Obviously, Poe had picked up on the sparks flying between him and Jamie. She'd have to work harder to smother that connection.

"I know that we only have one shot to achieve our goal because our target is leaving for a holiday on Monday." He shook his head. "Can you imagine? He is the only surgeon who has the ability to do this surgery and he dares to take a vacation." He laughed. "Doesn't say a whole lot for his level of compassion."

"You ever heard of burnout?" Poe tossed back at him.

Both men had a point. "All right," Jamie said, redirecting the conversation. "So we have to get him during the party on Sunday night or risk him getting away before he can do what your employer needs him to do."

"*Our* employer," Abi countered.

"What's the plan to get into the house?" Poe asked.

"You don't need that information yet," Abi said. "You will learn each step as needed. That's the most secure way to move forward."

She and Poe exchanged a frustrated look.

"For now, there are other security issues that need to be addressed. I'll need your cell phones and we'll conduct a little pat down."

"You can't be serious." Jamie shook her head. "No way."

Abi turned his hands up. "It's your choice but you know the consequences."

"Fine." She passed him her cell. There was no option for resisting. "Just do it."

With visible reluctance, Poe held out his cell phone as well.

Abi took the phones to the coffee table, gave them a

quick check and then added what was no doubt a tracking device or bug of some sort.

"You are to make no unauthorized calls until this is done." He handed each one their phone back. "You are not to leave this house until the job is finished."

"I take it you're here to stay." Not really a question in Jamie's opinion. He was here for the duration, she suspected.

"I will be here until you complete this mission."

"Look me in the eye," Jamie demanded, "and tell me that you do not have orders to terminate anyone when this is over." Not that she was afraid of him getting the upper hand on her. She wasn't. She was every bit as good as he was one-on-one. But she was worried about what might happen to her brother even if she did get the doctor. And his family. Would Case's family be harmed? As for Poe, like her, he could take care of himself.

"I have no termination orders," Abi said. "Unless, you fail to follow through with your instructions and, I will be honest with you, I declined that part of the deal. If you opt out or fail, your brother's execution will be carried out by someone else, but mark my word, it will be carried out."

She supposed she couldn't ask for more than full disclosure.

"There is just one issue," Abi said.

Here it came. Damn it.

"Your friend here," Abi said with a glance at Poe. "He was not part of the plan."

Poe visibly braced.

"Which means," Abi said, "that I have the less than pleasant duty of informing my employer of the modification."

"Please," Jamie said bluntly, "you have had ample time to do this already. Obviously, you had a clue it was happening because you provided clothes for him."

"Actually, those are mine."

Jamie held up both hands. Oh. She hadn't thought of that. "Whatever. I want Poe here. He's with me—to watch my back. Deal with it."

She held her breath. Hoped to hell he would allow her this one concession.

For a long moment, Abi only stared at her. Finally, he looked away. "You're lucky I'm feeling generous." He shrugged. "Besides, we might need him for a distraction of some sort if we get into trouble."

"I don't plan to get into trouble," Jamie argued. "That's your MO, not mine."

Abi laughed. "Well, let's hope you can keep that record. This is not going to be as easy as it sounds."

The fact that he had inside information compelled her to believe him. "Tell me about the hard parts."

"Dr. Case has a body double."

Dread dragged at her gut. "Are you serious?"

"I am indeed. The most difficult part will be making sure we take the right guy and that we keep his wife and daughter out of the line of fire."

What kind of doctor hired a body double?

"You have some way of proving who the real Dr. Case is?" God, she hoped so. Because all she had was a photo of the man.

"I do and it's foolproof. But that doesn't mean he will make this easy."

Jamie shrugged. "It doesn't have to be easy. It just has to be doable."

She would do whatever necessary to save her brother's life—even give up her own.

"It is doable," Abi said.

"No more issues with or questions about Poe," she pressed.

Abi shook his head. "I will handle the situation."

Poe scoffed. "Somehow I figured that was the answer all along, otherwise you might have to get your hands dirty."

Abi chuckled. "You might be smarter than I anticipated."

The standoff lasted about five seconds. Poe said, "You mentioned a pat down." He gestured to Abi. "Why don't we get that part over with? Jamie and I like to know who we're working with—what he carries, what he's hiding. Things like that. You want to go first?"

Jamie rolled her eyes. *Let the games begin.*

Saturday, December 22

Three Days Before Christmas

Chapter Four

Excalibur Court,
8:30 a.m.

Jamie wiped the steam from the mirror. The shower had cleared her head a bit. She'd barely slept last night. She couldn't stop thinking about Luke and how he must be feeling.

Her little brother was a good guy. His need to help others was so clear in his every decision. The fact that he wanted to be a doctor said so much about him. She had to make sure he came through this safely. No one should be kidnapped and held against his will, but Luke was one of the last people on the planet who deserved such treatment. Jamie wished she could claim credit for even ten percent of his good works. The man was always donating his time and/or ability to one cause or another.

There had been times when Jamie worried that this made him vulnerable. It wasn't that she didn't agree with the work he did, but he had to be more careful to protect himself. He was a Colby. This made him a target far more so than he wanted to admit. She'd warned him time and time again that he had to be careful. He shouldn't just blindly trust anyone.

She scrubbed the towel over her skin. That wasn't fair.

Just because he had been targeted and taken hostage did not mean he hadn't been careful.

When she'd dried her body and whipped her hair into a damp ponytail, she put on the jeans and sweatshirt that had been provided. Her host had thought of everything. Clothes. Shoes. Toiletries. The scariest part was that these were toiletries she would have chosen.

She suspected Abi had taken care of those details or at least helped with that part. Or maybe he'd been the one to think of it period. He was quite a diva when it came to personal comfort. No matter. She had carefully checked every single item for tracking devices and anything else that could be used to monitor her movements or subdue her in any way. As she'd done so, her mind had conjured images of her and Abi together...their bodies entwined.

She rolled her eyes and put the thought out of her head. She knew firsthand how he liked things. She and Abi had a thing for a little while late last year. It hadn't been a big deal. She'd run into him after a long and exhausting assignment. She'd had a feeling he'd picked her out of the pack and zeroed in on her. Maybe she was being paranoid, but it had felt that way. There were plenty of others in the agency he could have targeted.

Of course, his decision to go after her had nothing to do with this current mission.

She gave her reflection one last look. There were several items on her to-do list today and she wasn't standing for Abi getting in her way. He might be in charge of babysitting, but this was her op.

When she opened the bedroom door, the smell of coffee had her ready to moan. The house was a large one with five bedrooms—each with its own bath—and a large center great room with its impressive balcony and telescope. Oh, and the infinity pool was inspiring even in the window. The steam rising from it this morning told her it was heated.

"Good morning, sleeping beauty," Abi announced as bread popped out of the toaster.

"Who slept?" she grumbled. She felt confident her grandparents hadn't slept last night either. Like her, they were probably terrified for Luke. She hadn't been able to stop thinking about him.

She stilled, then glanced around the room. "Where's Poe?"

"He's having a look around outside. Checking out the ride that's been provided to you."

Of course he was. *Men.* "I have some things to do."

Abi passed her a plate loaded with toast, each slice smeared with a plop of guacamole. "Great. I'll go with you. Poe can hold down the fort."

"Sorry, but where I go, Poe goes." The toast actually looked quite good. He'd chopped up tomatoes and sprinkled them across the top. She took a bite. This time she did moan.

"You need coffee."

As if it hadn't been fourteen months, two weeks and three days since they'd seen each other, he prepared her a cup of coffee with exactly the right amount of almond milk creamer.

"What is it you want, Abi?" He was up to something. This was another thing that had kept her awake last night. It wasn't like him to be so attentive unless he wanted something more than he'd stated. Then again, she supposed it was his job to keep her focused and content until the job was done. Whatever the case, trust was not something she would be tossing out for him.

"It's my job to ensure you have everything you need and are fully prepared for the op."

She decided the coffee was too good to spoil with a long conversation, so she ate her toast and drank it while it was hot. When she finished her coffee, she asked the burning question. "Why aren't you doing the job? Why kidnap my brother and force me to do something I'm sure you can do yourself?" They had talked about this last night and the trust issue, but she still wasn't convinced he'd been completely forthcoming on the subject.

Abi sipped his coffee and appeared to consider her question. "My employer wants the best and I assured him you are the very best. Think about it—this is not the sort of situation you wish to leave to chance."

"Your employer has a family member who has an inoperable brain tumor." It wasn't a question. They had tiptoed around this issue yesterday too.

"What's on your agenda?" Abi asked, ignoring her question. "You mentioned things you needed to do."

She considered the man and wondered what in his life had formed his decision to go down this murky path. His father had been a high-ranking member of the Mossad and after retirement, his role in Israeli politics became noteworthy. But Abi had been raised by his mother in London and he had not chosen to serve either country in any capacity. He served only himself.

"Initial stop—my brother's condo. I want to have a look around."

"You believe there's something more going on than what you've been told in your briefing?"

She took her cup and plate to the sink. If he was expecting her to do the dishes because he had cooked, he could forget it. "I don't believe or disbelieve anything. I simply wish to have a look at my brother's home."

He gave a nod. "As you wish."

"Later we can go over the plan." She might as well understand how his employer expected this to go down.

"We won't be going over the plan until we are ready to move."

This she found troubling. "You're assuming there's no room for error in your plan. How can you be so sure the plan doesn't need to be tweaked?"

"The plan is perfect."

"There's no such thing as a perfect plan," she argued.

He smiled. "I'll agree to disagree."

The door opened and Poe joined them in the kitchen. "Morning." He looked from her to Abi and back. "Everything okay?"

"We're going to Luke's condo to have a look around."

He nodded, his expression giving nothing of his feelings away. "Can we talk for a minute?"

"Sure."

"Let's take a walk," Poe suggested. "Outside."

"Sure." She flashed a smile for Abi. "We'll be just outside." She wanted a look around out there anyway.

On the way out the door, Jamie grabbed her coat—the one provided with the other items for this op. Poe had nothing but the windbreaker he'd been wearing in LA. Not exactly suitable for December in Tennessee.

Once they were outside and walking around the infinity pool overlooking the wooded valley below, Poe turned to her. "What's the deal between you and this guy?"

With all that was going on, this was what he needed to talk about?

"Nothing." She surveyed the valley and the house that sat in the middle of those woods. The house was their target. Getting in and out of there with the surgeon in tow would never be easy. Whatever Abi thought, the sort of man who had a body double on staff no doubt had serious protection wherever he went. He would not go with Jamie willingly.

On top of the idea that there was a good chance they would end up dead just for trying to get to him, there was the idea of what would happen if they were successful. The authorities wouldn't rest until they solved the case. Beyond that, there was the concern that the surgeon could end up injured or dead.

Luke could end up injured or dead.

So many things could go wrong.

"Come on, Jamie. I can see there's a connection. How do you know this guy?"

"I bumped into him late last year after an assignment for the agency. He attempted to infiltrate my cover. The op was over, so I don't know why he bothered. Maybe just to see if he could. To flirt."

Poe held up his hands. "Maybe I don't want to know." He visibly shook himself. Maybe from the cold. "So I've thought about the layout down there." He looked toward the surgeon's home. "The security protocols he used the last time he hosted a party and his personal security team are detailed in the package Abi provided. The chances of getting in and out of there will be slim. Very slim." He shook his head. "I have a really bad feeling about this."

She smiled sadly. "It's not like I have a choice. I have to try."

"I did some research on Case as well. He's not exactly known as Mr. Personality. I don't think your friend's employer understands that he could very well refuse to do the surgery."

Jamie had considered this could be an issue. "I suppose we'll just have to convince him somehow."

"But we can't make him," Poe argued. "We can put a

gun to his head, but we cannot make him do the surgery. Torturing him or shooting him won't be an option."

"You're saying you don't think the plan is a good one."

He moved his head from side to side. "The doctor will need proper motivation."

Jamie thought of the photos of the doctor and his family she had reviewed. "He has a kid. A little girl."

Poe nodded. "Ten years old. Take the kid for leverage and there won't be any trouble getting him to go along with whatever he's asked to do. I'm guessing that's why Abi isn't sharing more details. He knows you aren't going to like it."

Fury roared through Jamie. "On top of that, it's another reason why he isn't doing this on his own. He'll focus on the kid while you and I whisk away the surgeon."

"That's what I'm thinking. There's a hell of a lot of room for error, especially with a kid in the mix. I don't like this, Jamie."

She swore. She hated when people used kids for leverage. "I don't either."

A quick review of their options was pretty straightforward: do as they were told or do as they were told. "We'll go with the plan as far as we can," she said, feeling suddenly tired. "From there, we'll do what we have to do to ensure everyone survives."

"This friend of yours," Poe said. "Any suspicions he'll double cross us when the job is done?"

"There's always that chance. We just need to be ready for anything that comes our way."

Jamie's attention shifted to the house. Abi was watching them from the other side of the wall of glass. He knew a lot more than he was sharing.

The question was, would it get them killed?

Douglas Avenue,
10:20 a.m.

LUKE'S CONDO WAS a wreck. And as much as Luke despised housecleaning, this was more than just his indifference to chores. The place had been ransacked. She shouldn't be surprised, and she wasn't. Not really. More unsettled. This was Luke's place. His things.

Jamie moved through the condo slowly, taking her time to look at any and all items. The space wasn't that large so with both Poe and Abi prowling around it was on the cramped side.

She tidied the place as she went. Touching Luke's things relieved her somehow. Relaxed her to a degree. He was her little brother. She loved him. She'd always taken care of him.

"There were three of them," Poe said. "Two who pilfered through his things, one who interrogated him."

Jamie hoped the interrogation hadn't included any torture. "I haven't spotted any blood."

Poe shook his head. "Me either."

This was good. She watched as Poe moved around the space, pausing to linger and then tracing his fingers over an item. Poe read crime scenes like no one she had ever met. Just being in the room and touching the victim's things could pull him in deep enough to practically see through the eyes of the victim.

It was an uncanny gift.

Jamie moved on to her brother's bedroom and picked through his things. She tidied what she could and made a pile of what should be in the laundry hamper.

"Finding anything relevant?"

She turned to find Abi propped in the open doorway. "Nothing yet."

"It doesn't appear anything—including your brother—was damaged in the search."

"The question is, why did they need to search? If my brother was simply leverage, what were they looking for?"

"Perhaps—" Abi pushed away from the door and walked deeper into the room "—he refused to cooperate with their questions about you."

"So they were looking through his underwear drawers for information on my whereabouts?"

A smirk twitched Abi's lips. "One never knows about siblings."

"Ha ha." She smiled at the framed photo on the dresser. The fam—their mom and dad and the two of them. If anything had happened to Luke...

No, she couldn't go there.

"I'm sure you knew how to find me," she said as she exited the room.

Abi followed. "I suppose I should have mentioned as much."

"You weren't here when they picked up Luke?"

"I'm afraid not."

That explained the search.

"Did you suggest they use my brother as leverage?" The thought made her furious. She clamped her jaw shut to prevent saying more than she should. Staying on good terms was imperative—at least for now. She could punch him in the face later. When this was done.

He made a big deal of appearing to consider her question. "I may have suggested the concept."

She so wanted to kick his butt.

"Well, at least now I know who ruined my Christmas."

She put the pile of soiled clothes in the hamper and walked to the kitchen. She took her time and had a look around. She didn't really expect to find anything useful here, but she would be remiss if she didn't go through the steps. At the front door, she paused to open the coat closet. She picked through the offerings until she found something suitable for Poe.

"You need this more than the windbreaker." She passed the leather coat to him.

"Thanks."

She turned to Abi. "Where are they keeping him?"

"I'm afraid I have no idea."

Probably a lie. "Why can't I see him? Verify that he's okay."

"You'll see him when the op is complete. You have my word that he is okay."

"Is that supposed to make me feel better?" This man would say whatever he was paid to say. They both knew this to be true.

"I would certainly hope so." He looked from her to Poe and back. "Are we ready to go back to the house?"

Jamie walked to her brother's desk and sat down. She tapped the trackpad to wake the computer. It was up and running and required a password. She didn't attempt to access the system. No need. Her brother was too smart to leave information too readily accessible. She opened the two shallow drawers and picked through them. Nothing of particular interest. Sharpies, pens. She hadn't really expected there to be anything helpful as to his whereabouts, but she wanted to buy time. She was in no hurry to get back to the Excalibur house. But there was one other thing she wanted to find out.

"I'm finished." She stood, pushed in her chair and headed for the door.

They locked up and descended the stairs that led down

to the ground level. Jamie surveyed the street and postage-stamp-size yard that served two condos. The place was like her brother—efficient, well thought out, minimal. He didn't like wasting time. And he didn't like a lot of stuff.

Jamie settled into the passenger seat while Abi slid behind the steering wheel. Poe climbed in the back. She was sure he wasn't very happy about being relegated to the back seat, but someone had to take one for the team.

"We should stop for lunch." She shrugged. "Since we're out, I mean." Mostly, she just didn't want to rush back to the house. And she'd like to see if anyone was following them. She hadn't spotted anyone on the way here. Going back might be a different story.

Nashville was not Abi's home turf. Jamie knew far more about this city than he did—only because her brother lived here. Despite being in charge, out here in the wild, Abi was just one of them.

"Why my brother and why me?" The story he'd given her up to now just didn't fit in her opinion.

"Your reputation precedes you," he said, absorbed in navigating traffic.

"I'm still not buying it."

There was something he was leaving out. Something relevant. And even if there wasn't, it kept him trying to assuage her concerns. She liked making him work for his comfort.

"Perhaps it's best not to dwell on the whys and just do what we must do."

"How did he find you?"

He glanced at her. Now there was a question he hadn't been expecting. "I have a certain reputation."

This was true. "What're you doing? Advertising on the dark web now?"

"I shouldn't answer that question."

Keeping an eye on the exterior mirror on her side, she said, "I'm still not convinced of why they need us both." She and Poe had discussed the idea of Dr. Case's child being a target as well, which would certainly require more than one pair of hands.

But it didn't have to be Jamie or her brother.

"We'll have food delivered to the house," he said as he pointed the car in that direction.

And there it was. This other thing that nagged at her. He wanted to keep her at the house until it was time for the op. Was he concerned something would happen? That she would be injured somehow, making her useless for the purposes of the operation?

As if fate had decided to answer her question, a black sedan appeared in the passenger-side mirror. It was a ways back, but she watched as he made turn after turn and the sedan did the same. Oh yeah. They had a tail.

"Does having me here have something to do with my grandmother?" She hadn't considered the idea until now. The Colby name was internationally known. Mostly she was making conversation while she watched their tail.

"This only has to do with you and your participation in achieving the proper outcome. Trying to read something more into it is a waste of time."

He was sticking to his story, which suggested he could possibly be telling the truth.

But she wasn't ready to let him off the hook just yet.

"Your father was kidnapped as a child."

The question startled her. Jamie glanced back at Poe. He knew about what her father had gone through. They were friends. Good friends. She'd shared more with him than she did with most. She shifted her attention to the driver.

But she hadn't shared any of that with this man. Finding this information wouldn't be so difficult, but the question was why did he consider it relevant enough to look into?

"He was. He was taken at seven years old and wasn't found until more than two decades later. My grandparents thought he was dead, so they had stopped looking."

"You know what happened to him during that time?"

"Why are we talking about this?" Poe demanded.

"It's okay," she said to her friend. Then, to Abi, she said, "I do. Why do you ask?" To say this line of questioning was making her tense was an understatement. She did not like the idea of feeling a comparison between her father's and her brother's kidnapping situations. No one who knew those circumstances would.

"No reason. I was just curious."

That was a lie. Until just this minute, she hadn't really considered who his employer was. Now she was more than a little concerned. Was he somehow connected to her family? Or their past?

She suddenly wished she could speak to her dad.

"You ask a lot of questions," Poe said, likely noting her uneasiness.

Abi laughed. "Curiosity killed the cat."

He made a sharp turn and then gunned the accelerator. Oh, she got it now. He wanted to distract them from the fact that they had a tail.

"You got some idea of who our tail is?" She looked to Abi for his answer.

His jaw hardened. He never took failure well. "Not to worry. We will lose him."

"Are you sure?"

He sent her a hard look and then took another treacherous turn.

This was a secret mission with a secret target and a secret benefactor. Who else could know their plan? At first, Jamie had wondered if it was part of some security detail. It didn't appear to be someone Abi wanted on their tail.

As they drove, seemingly tail-free now, he watched the mirrors closely. Took several more unnecessary turns in Jamie's opinion. She thought of the doctor—their target. He was just a man, but one with very special talents. At this time there was no one else like him in what he could do. He was uniquely necessary to fulfill a need that could be fulfilled no other way.

What was that ability worth? A lot, apparently. Enough to go to great lengths to make this happen.

There was still something—a piece she was missing. Perhaps it was irrelevant in the grand scheme of things, but she couldn't shake the nagging sensation that there was something more she needed to know...to understand.

Poe could feel it too. She saw it in his eyes whenever they grilled Abi this way.

Jamie made a decision. She had to ask this burning question. "Before we move into position for the op, I'll need to know the part you're not telling me."

Abi laughed. "You should let this foolish idea go. You have my word, Jamie. There is nothing else to know."

Funny, that did not make her feel one iota better.

"And that answer," she said, glancing at him, "is why I will never trust you, Abi."

"You can trust me, Jamie. This is a simple matter of monumental importance. That's all. The weight of the concept is misleading on a basic implementation level. Don't overthink it."

The man so loved throwing those opposing adjectives together.

"I hope you're being straight with me, Abi. I don't want either of us to regret this thing you've decided we must do."

He flashed her one of those grins that made breathing difficult. "No regrets."

Then why did she feel as if she regretted it already?

Chapter Five

Abi excused himself and went outside to take a call.

He hadn't stopped for food. But Jamie got why he hadn't.

"I don't like this." Poe stared beyond the wall of glass doors and watched Abi pace back and forth next to the infinity pool.

Jamie braced her hands on her hips and met her friend's gaze. "I'm with you, believe me. If something is going wrong this early in the game, we're in trouble."

"You're thinking of that tail he struggled to lose."

She nodded. "That was my primary reason for wanting to go out today. He's making this all seem so pat—as if everything is in place with no concerns. This—" she looked to the man outside "—is a concern."

Poe turned his back to the outdoor space and fixed his worried gaze on Jamie. "You know when you have this feeling deep in your gut that something is really, really wrong but you can't quite put your finger on the problem?"

Jamie flattened her palm against her belly. "Right here. The same place that lets you know when you need to cut and run."

"Yeah." He glanced over his shoulder at the man outside. "I'm not saying your friend is setting us up, but he knows this is off somehow and he's just going along as if it's all good."

Yeah, she'd picked up on that. "The good news is I didn't get the impression at Luke's place that there was a truly violent struggle or any of the usual issues we should worry about."

Actually, that could be good or bad, but she had decided to see it as a good thing. Victoria had heard Luke's voice. For now, the situation appeared to be running along without any glitches—with the exception of the potential tail they'd had to lose. If the plan played out the way they had been briefed, then hopefully Luke would be released tomorrow night.

She wasn't thinking beyond that. It wasn't like a person or persons could be kidnapped and everyone involved just walked away as if nothing had happened. There would be repercussions. And, frankly, it wasn't like she could pretend she had immunity in the kidnapping of a prestigious doctor—if this went down as planned.

Since Abi appeared in no hurry to get back inside, Jamie decided to use the time wisely. Who knew how much time she and Poe would have alone?

"What do we know about this Dr. Case?" Poe asked. "I mean, really? Beyond the bio on his website and in the file Abi provided?"

"I was just thinking the same thing," Jamie admitted. "The basics are that he graduated from Vanderbilt, then went on to specialize at Johns Hopkins. He spent the next dozen years building his claim to fame in neurosurgery."

Poe glanced outside to ensure Abi remained preoccupied. "Early this year he completed the first successful surgery removing a previously deemed inoperable brain tumor. Since that time, he's completed many more such operations. But he's only one man."

"And patients from all over the country are frantically trying to get on his schedule."

"While he," Poe said, "is talking about cutting back on the number of surgeries he's doing in order to train more surgeons to do the same."

"But the patients are desperate—they're facing death sentences without this surgery." Jamie started to pace. She could only imagine how the patients felt. If the doctor was doing all he could, then this wasn't easy for him either.

"The bottom line is," Poe went on, "what does your friend's employer want with Dr. Case?"

"Ostensibly, this lifesaving surgery for himself or a family member."

"Either way, the man—woman, whoever—has the means to go after what he wants no matter that it's not legal."

"He has the means but he doesn't have the time to wait," Jamie agreed. "So he's buying a place at the front of the line." Certainly not fair but there were those who would do whatever necessary to get what they wanted.

"If he's smart he has created a plan that ensures he will walk away from this without revealing his identity." Poe shrugged. "It's the only possibility that makes sense. Why would he want to live only to go to prison?"

"Which suggests it's a family member, so he doesn't care." Jamie frowned. "The one hitch in that plan is the doctor. How does Abi's employer protect his identity from the surgeon himself?"

"I don't see how he can." Poe considered the idea for a moment. "Unless it's all carefully choreographed in a way that Case does his thing and then he's taken away. The employer's personal physician will take it from there. Which would mean he'd require a private surgery suite."

"Why the Colby Agency?" Jamie shrugged. "I mean, the agency is the best, but there are other players out there who could help with this op. I haven't seen or heard anything as of yet that makes me believe I have a particular skill set that this guy couldn't find in another operative."

"But," Poe said with a look that underscored his words, "it's you this guy—" he hitched a thumb toward Abi "—wanted to play with."

She couldn't deny the possibility. "Maybe, but Abi is smart. He wouldn't allow his personal feelings to get in the way of a successful mission. He's too good for that."

"Then we have to assume there's a personal connection between your family and this mission. Or perhaps that's what he wants us to believe."

That was the part that worried Jamie. Which was true?

"I need to have a closer look around here." She surveyed the large great room. "Can you keep Abi preoccupied when he comes back in while I have a look around?"

"Sure. We'll just pretend to be mates," he teased in a faux British accent.

Jamie shook her head at her friend, glanced toward Abi and then hurried out of the room. She made her way up the stairs and went straight to the bedroom Abi had chosen for himself. He'd made the room assignments. Considering the clothing and toiletry selections he'd prepared for her, he'd had access to this property for at least a day or two before they arrived.

She opened the door and walked into his room. The bed was unmade. The rumpled sheets kept her gaze lingering longer than they should have. She forced her attention to the nightstands next to the bed. She quickly went through the drawers of each. The only personal item she found was a cell phone charger. She moved on to the dresser where she rummaged through his underwear and socks, taking care to feel for any items that might be hidden inside.

She found nothing in the drawers or under them, so the closet was next. Two blazers and three shirts hung on wooden hangers. Jamie checked the pockets and then the extra pair of shoes standing neatly on the carpet.

There was nothing in the room that he wouldn't want anyone to find.

Jamie walked out of his room and closed the door the way she had found it. Abi was too savvy to leave anything lying around that might give away some aspect of his plan. She went through her and Poe's rooms, double-checking for bugs. She found nothing.

Downstairs, Abi had come inside.

"Since we weren't able to stop, I'll order lunch," he announced.

Jamie wasn't sure she could eat, but she kept that to herself. Food was essential to gain energy. "Anything but pizza." She had eaten pizza two nights in a row on the previous mission.

Poe laughed. "Yeah, the only food available near that last motel was pizza."

"No pizza," Abi assured them. "I was thinking Mediterranean."

"Works for me," Poe announced.

"I need to check in with Victoria," Jamie announced. She needed to know what was going on.

Abi looked up from whatever app he'd chosen to use for ordering food. "As long as I can hear the conversation, I don't have a problem with that."

Jamie nodded. "Understood."

Poe caught her gaze. "I think I'll take a nap until the food comes."

Sounded like Poe had some looking around he wanted to do as well. He disappeared upstairs, and Jamie put through the call. Her grandmother answered on the first ring. "It's me," Jamie said, wishing she could be there in person to talk to her. She'd likely been waiting for a call all day.

"Are you okay, Jamie?"

She smiled. She loved the sound of her grandmother's voice. So commanding and yet so caring. "I'm good, yes. We went to Luke's condo today. I didn't find any readily visible cause for alarm."

"Have you spoken to him?"

"No. Maybe I'll get to later." Jamie chewed her lower lip. There was a lot she wanted to say but holding back was the smarter choice. "Any news from Mom and Dad?"

Her mother hadn't been herself lately. Jamie was glad she and Dad were on vacation and not in the middle of this mess.

"I did," Victoria said. "They're doing well. Just missing all of us. I assured them we will all be fine for Christmas. They should enjoy themselves and relax."

"That's exactly what they should do," Jamie agreed. "I hope you gave them my love."

"I certainly did. Jamie…"

She heard the worry in her grandmother's voice. "Really, Grandmother, I'm fine."

"Please be careful. I wish there was more we could do."

"Knowing that you're standing by is enough."

They talked a few minutes more before Jamie was able to say goodbye. She so loved her grandparents. Victoria was the epitome of all that Jamie believed was right in this world. She hoped to be able to accomplish just a fraction of what her grandmother had done with her life. Her grandfather too.

"What's the ETA on the food?" She tucked her cell phone away.

"Should be here any minute." Abi searched her face, her eyes. "I find it difficult to believe your grandparents aren't up to something. But I haven't picked up on any chatter from the Colby Agency."

"They would never do anything that might endanger Luke or me."

"You're lucky to have people who care about you that way."

She felt like that was an opening, but decided not to take it. "I'll find Poe. Let him know the food will be here soon."

Giving Abi her back, she hurried from the room and up the stairs. She found Poe in his room, staring out the window toward the home of Dr. Quentin Case.

"Abi says the food will be here soon."

Poe glanced at her, then waited for her to join him at the window. "I can't figure out what he thinks he's accomplishing by keeping everything a secret until the last minute. You know there's a reason that we're not going to like."

"I know." She leaned one shoulder against the window frame. "The only reason to do that is if he thinks I'll have an issue with the proposed execution of the op."

"The house is right there." He nodded in the direction of the mansion in the valley below. "Why not just spell it out now? It's not like we can't put together a number of scenarios in our heads. We've done this sort of thing too many times."

"Maybe he's worried we'll give him the slip and share the details with the police or with someone else who can stop him." This wasn't the sort of global issue the IOA dealt with, but they would certainly not hesitate to send an extraction team to recover two of their agents. Except contacting anyone at all was a risk she wasn't willing to take. Luke's life hung in the balance.

"Unless," Poe countered, "the employer is Abi himself."

Now this was an avenue she had not considered. "You may be right." Wow. She knew Abi's family. There was his father. His mother. No siblings. No spouse as far as she knew.

"Whatever he's planning," Poe said, drawing her attention back to him, "I don't want you taking the risk too far. You have to protect yourself, Jamie."

She frowned. "Why would I not protect myself? It's the first rule of any op. You can't complete it if you're down for the count."

Poe laughed. "You always do that. Deflect. I just don't want you to throw caution to wind for this guy. He's not worth it, Jamie. He's using you and Luke."

Yeah. She recognized Poe was right on that one. "I'm aware."

He reached up and tucked a strand of hair behind her ear. "You're important to me, Jamie. Our work is sometimes dangerous—maybe not so much when we're plucking Santas from trouble."

She laughed. "Even Santa needs rescuing sometimes."

"True. Just be careful. I don't trust this guy at all."

She hugged him. Closed her eyes and inhaled deeply of his unique scent. "Don't worry. I plan on taking you home for Christmas when this is finished."

She'd made that decision the moment this whole thing started. She wanted her family to know this man. The realization surprised her a little…but in a good way.

10:00 p.m.

JAMIE STOOD ON the patio and stared toward the Case home. The place was lit up like an airfield. If the family had company tonight, it wasn't obvious. No cars parked in the front cobblestoned parking area. Even from here she could see the massive fountain with its flickering lights that sat in the middle of that parking area.

According to Google, the house where Dr. Case lived had only been built two years ago to the tune of several million dollars. He'd built the house even before perfecting the surgical procedure that had put him on the map. He had two children. A son who had started Harvard this past fall. And a daughter who was only ten years old. His wife wrote children's books and spent a lot of time volunteering. Good for her. She was also a nurse, but she donated her time to a clinic in downtown Nashville.

By all accounts, the family was highly respected and more than a little revered in the area.

All the more reason for Jamie to see this through one way or another. Someone had to protect that family during this… Whatever it was. She just hoped she wasn't going to be caught in a situation where she had to choose between her brother and a member of the doctor's family.

So far there had been no mention of weapons, but she wasn't naive enough to believe they were going into this thing unarmed. Particularly considering Case had serious security. There would be weapons, and anytime weapons were involved, trouble was just one tiny mistake away.

That would be the problem. Getting in and out without triggering a gunfight with the doctor's security team.

As if she'd voiced the issue out loud, Abi joined her

on the patio. He surveyed the valley below before turning to her.

"It's cold out here," he pointed out.

Her body suddenly realized he was right. She shivered. "I hadn't noticed."

He laughed. "I see that."

She wrapped her arms around herself. "Not that cold. Remember I grew up in Chicago."

He removed the jacket he was wearing and draped it over her shoulders. "I remember."

The warmth from his body immediately seeped into hers. "Thanks." She tugged the coat closer around her.

"Your friend has been pacing the floor for hours."

Poe had paced the floor down here until only a few minutes ago and then he'd called it a night only to pace the floor in his room.

"He's restless."

"He needs to chill." Abi crossed his arms over his chest, the cold night air obviously getting to him since he'd given his jacket to her.

"Maybe he could if you'd give us some insight into how this is going down."

"I'm afraid I can't do that. You will know exactly what to do when it's time to move."

She heaved a frustrated breath. "That's no way to run a railroad," she argued. "Preparation is always key in any operation. Preparation of all players."

He shot her a grin. "Trust me. I have thoroughly prepared for this. For all of us."

"Tell me one thing." She turned to him and fixed her gaze on his.

"One thing," he agreed.

"Does someone in your family need this doctor's help?"

If this was personal, the situation was all the more danger-ous. Personal was never, ever good.

"No one in my family is involved. This is not personal, Jamie. You have my word."

"Good." She considered what she should ask next. "How did you learn of this mission?"

"So what you really want is two things," he said, eye-brows raised.

"The one thing was just me getting started."

He smiled. "I see that." He exhaled an audible breath. "I was approached by a representative of my employer."

He looked directly at her as he spoke. Gaze open. No blink, no flinch. So far he appeared to be telling her the truth.

"Are you completely comfortable with the plan?" She had worked with Abi before. He was good. Damned good.

"The plan is flawless. You do not need to worry about the plan. I have considered every possibility. There are no weaknesses...no holes."

"Your reputation is impeccable when it comes to plan-ning and executing a mission," Jamie confessed. "I saw firsthand when we worked together how capable you are."

"Capable." He chuckled. "A good word, I suppose."

"No other aspect of anyone's ability is relevant if it's not capable."

He seemed to weigh her words a moment. "We spent a good deal of time together during that mission."

They had spent a considerable amount of time together, and they had shared a *moment*.

The memory had her cheeks heating. She was thank-ful it was dark to prevent him seeing that she'd blushed at the memory.

"We worked well together," he pointed out.

"We did, but—" Jamie looked directly at him "—it can't be like last time."

Her brother's life was in the balance. She could not allow herself to be distracted.

"The mission hasn't started yet," he argued. "Who knows what we'll find time for before we're finished?"

"Did you drag my brother into this just so you could force me to be involved?"

"How do you know Luke isn't my employer?"

The question startled her. This was something she had not considered. She thought a moment about the possibility. To her knowledge, Luke had no significant other just now. He would have told her. But she couldn't say with complete certainty that there wasn't someone he wanted to help. He was always doing things for other people—especially those in need. This seemed a little over-the-top for his ability. He had a sizable trust fund, but it wasn't like he could withdraw that kind of money without permission.

Unless that was what the ten-million-dollar ransom was about.

The thought had her gritting her teeth for a moment. No, she decided. No way.

"Luke would have come to me if he'd needed help with something like this." Jamie was certain. He wouldn't have gone about it this way. No way.

Abi searched her face, her eyes. "I did not and would not have taken your brother hostage in order to get your attention. It's important that you understand that was not my decision."

"Can you guarantee me he's safe?"

"I can assure you that he is perfectly safe."

"Then you trust your employer enough to take that risk?"

He frowned. "What risk?"

"The risk that if something happens to my brother, I will make you pay."

His frown slid into a grin. "I am very well aware of what would happen to me if I was responsible for trouble with your brother."

"Just so you know, I won't go in without being fully briefed and feeling confident that all is as it should be. So don't go suggesting it's time to go with the idea of filling me in on the way. I will refuse."

"I'm aware." He tugged the lapels of the jacket a little closer to ensure she stayed warm. "We will go through everything very carefully before we move in."

So they were invading the house.

"I'm assuming we have invitations to the party," she said, mostly just to see what he would say.

"Better to be invited than to have to figure out another way in."

"Your employer is powerful."

"Of course."

That he was rich went without saying. "But he isn't powerful enough to get the one thing he wants more than anything else."

Abi's gaze collided with hers. "There are some things even money cannot buy."

Which told her that Abi's employer had already approached this doctor and been turned away.

"For all those other things," Jamie suggested, "there are people like you."

Abi smiled. "If not me, someone else would do it. At least if I do it, I do it well."

No question. The upside was that what she knew of Abi was as close to good as a mostly bad guy could be.

"I know what you're thinking."

She sort of hoped he did not. "And what's that?"

"You're thinking 'What is a bad guy like me doing trying to help someone do a good thing—like kidnap a doctor to save a life?'"

"The thought occurred to me, yes." It wasn't the usual job Abi was known for.

"You're wondering," he went on, "if I might be growing soft in my old age."

She laughed. She couldn't help herself. Abi was only thirty. "Didn't cross my mind."

"When I was approached about this mission," he explained, "I could not say no. By this time tomorrow you will understand my reasons."

"I'm sure you're aware that no one involved is going to walk away from this legally speaking." It wasn't a threat, merely a statement of fact.

"I have a plan for that as well."

He sounded so certain of himself. "I just hope your plan is as good as you seem to believe it is."

He traced a fingertip down her cheek before dropping his hand. "I have never failed. Never. You are aware of this."

She resisted the need to shiver at his touch. "Just because you've never failed doesn't mean you won't."

That was the part that worried her the most. There was always a first time for failure. And the first time was always the worst.

Chapter Six

Kenny stared out the window at the house below their position. He was more than a little worried about this operation. Not for himself, but for Jamie. And Luke. He didn't trust this guy Abidan Amar. At all.

He was aware of Amar before today. He'd heard Jamie talk about him, but only a couple of times. Now that he'd seen the two of them together, he understood why. They'd shared something when they did that operation together. No question about it. As ridiculous as it sounded, he was working hard not to look and sound as jealous as he felt, but it wasn't easy. If he was completely honest with himself, he would own the fact that he had very deep feelings for Jamie. But first and foremost, they were friends. Best friends. He didn't want to risk damaging that relationship. Not just because they worked together fairly often, but also because she meant a great deal to him. If necessary, he would gladly be just friends forever.

He thought of that one kiss they had shared. A smile tugged at his lips. It had actually been a part of the mission they were working together at the time. But he'd felt the connection as real as breathing. Good God, how he'd felt the connection. He'd been really careful since then. If a move happened between them, it would be because she initiated the action.

Jamie was the real deal, with an amazing family that he respected so much. She'd invited him to family celebrations on a number of occasions and it was during their shared downtime that he really felt the pull. Whatever happened, he was giving her plenty of space and plenty of time to make a move.

The sound of footfalls on the stairs told him she was coming up to the second floor. He moved soundlessly to the door and leaned against it. She hesitated outside his door and his heart bumped hard in his chest. Three seconds, then five elapsed before she went on into her room and closed the door. She'd wanted to say something or...

Give it a rest, Kenny.

Whatever she'd pondered during that brief pause, her sense of professionalism had prevented her from saying or doing whatever had crossed her mind.

For the best. For sure. This wasn't the time to get personal. Too much was unknown, and Luke's life hung in that precarious space of uncertainty.

Whatever this thing was that Abi was up to, Kenny would do everything in his power to protect Jamie and Luke. He almost laughed at the idea of Jamie needing him for protection. Backup, maybe. But she could certainly take care of herself and any jerk who would suggest otherwise did not know her at all.

Still, he worried that she trusted Amar far too much. Kenny didn't trust him one little bit. From that haughty accent of his to the way this whole thing was shaking down, Kenny didn't like it...at all.

He needed to sleep. He climbed into the bed and forced

his eyes closed. He thought of Jamie just across the hall. The way she smiled… The sound of her laugh. She was so beautiful and so smart.

If they got through this…maybe it was time he told her how he felt.

Maybe.

If he didn't lose his courage.

Sunday, December 23

Two Days Before Christmas

Chapter Seven

Excalibur Court,
7:00 a.m.

To her surprise Jamie had managed to sleep. Maybe sheer exhaustion had helped. Whatever the reasons, she was grateful to wake up somewhat refreshed. It was always easier to stay focused with a few hours of sleep under one's belt.

When she was a child, her grandmother had always warned that a lack of sleep stole one's waking life. Stole one's ability to function...to remember. Jamie had always taken sleep very seriously because of those warnings.

For the past hour she had been lying in her bed, mulling over the things Abi had said last night. He had a plan for not only getting the mission completed successfully but also for ensuring no one was arrested. She actually could not see how he planned to make that happen, but she could hope.

What they were about to do was illegal. Not just a little crime either. This was kidnapping. A felony. This wasn't the sort of dance on the edge you walked away so easily from. Though she might be able to argue that in her case she had no choice in the matter since her brother's life was at stake. She was, to a large degree, being forced to participate. Still, the powers that be would wonder why she hadn't called the proper authorities. Fear for her brother's safety was a fairly good defense. Their phones were monitored—no unauthorized calls. To go against that edict was to risk Luke's life. As for Abi, he was assuredly breaking numerous laws with no mitigating factors to provide relief. He no doubt expected to get away scot-free.

The Colby Agency had the best attorneys in the country but that worry wasn't a priority right now. Jamie wasn't really worried for her future. As long as she avoided shooting anyone, she could potentially see her way clear—legally speaking—of this business. Whatever happened, her endgame was to rescue her brother. Optimally, she would do this without harming anyone else or getting herself shot.

Keeping Poe out of trouble was her top priority next to rescuing Luke. She would not allow Poe to be hurt by this mess. When she'd come to bed last night, she had lingered outside his door. The need to talk to him, to just be with him had been almost overwhelming. But she had made the right decision.

They were good friends. Very good friends. Since that kiss, it had become harder and harder to pretend she didn't feel other things for him. But she didn't want to harm their friendship in any way.

Poe was the reason she'd been so vulnerable to Abi last year. Even before the kiss that she and Poe had shared, she'd been attracted to him. Funny how those things happened when you were least expecting them.

Get your head on straight, Jamie. After a quick shower, she tugged on the wardrobe selection for today. The fact that Abi had known what size jeans she wore wasn't such a big surprise. That he'd done so well selecting items she would feel comfortable in was an added plus. The sweatshirt sported a Chicago Cubs logo. She shook her head.

Nice of him to try to make her feel at home. She pulled on a pair of socks and the sneakers she'd worn from LA. She wondered if the Santa she and Poe had rescued fully understood yet that they had saved his life. Sometimes targets were so flustered about being plucked from whatever their circumstances that they never got that they were damned lucky to still be breathing.

She brushed her hair and pulled it into a ponytail. She and Poe needed to discuss a potential exit strategy—for him anyway. This wasn't really his fight and he needed to know she would understand if he ducked out.

But he wouldn't. She knew him too well. She and Poe had been friends for a while now. Good friends. She understood that if he had his way, they would take their relationship to the next level. He had never said as much and was fairly subtle about it, but the signs were unmistakable. Not happening. Jamie didn't want to risk what they had. It sounded cliché, but it was true. Falling in love wasn't on her agenda just now anyway.

She was young. They both were. They had plenty of time to fall in love. Her grandmother would be the first to say Jamie should stay focused on her career for now. All the rest could come later.

She removed her cell from its charger and tucked it into her hip pocket. Since this mission was to go down tonight, maybe Abi would be ready to share the details this morning. No matter that she wouldn't say as much, on some level she understood his hesitance. The sooner he shared the ins and outs of the mission, the sooner she and Poe could consider options for reacting differently than was intended. The sooner a leak could happen. He was just practicing extra careful precautions.

She walked to the door, leaned against it and listened.

All quiet. She eased the door open and looked both ways. Hall was clear. The distinct scent of coffee wafted from downstairs and had her leaning in that direction. But before going down, she wanted to see if Poe was still in his room.

Across the hall, she listened at his door. She didn't hear anything so she rapped softly on the door. "Poe," she whispered, "you up?"

Usually, he was up before her. It was possible he was already downstairs, but since she hadn't heard voices, she suspected not. She couldn't see him and Abi standing around in the kitchen staring at each other without exchanging at least a few words.

Then again, maybe she could see them glaring at each other, circling the room like two wrestlers about to tangle.

She knocked again and when no answer came, she opted to give the knob a turn and see if the door was locked. It was not. It opened with little effort. The room was empty. Bed unmade. No surprise there. Poe wasn't exactly the neatest dude on the planet. He would insist he had other assets, and he would be right. She had never met anyone who could read a scene the way he could. He almost had a sixth sense when it came to seeing the details. The FBI had wanted him so badly, but like her, Poe had wanted to do something different...something maybe more relevant.

Certainly, this operation had not been on either of their agendas.

Since the bathroom door stood partially open, she checked in there and found no sign of Poe. A towel hung over the shower door, suggesting he had showered before leaving the room or before bed last night. She wandered back into the hall. Maybe he had gone downstairs, and he and Abi actually were down there staring at each other, waiting to see who broke first.

Listening intently for any sign of life, she descended the stairs and made her way through the living room and into the kitchen.

No Poe. No Abi.

Then she spotted Abi on the patio, savoring his coffee. Steam rose from the mug he held, matching the steam wafting from the pool. He stared toward the house belonging to the doctor. She wondered if he was suffering second thoughts about what he had agreed to do.

Where the heck was Poe?

She made a full round of the first floor. Checked the powder room and the small library. She even had a look out the front windows. No Poe.

Worry started its slow creep around the edges of her mind. Poe wouldn't just leave without telling her where he was going. Besides, she was fairly confident that Abi wouldn't allow either of them to leave until this was done.

When she still found no sign of Poe, she opened the door onto the patio and joined Abi. "Good morning."

He gave her a nod. "Morning." He frowned. "No coffee?"

"I was looking for Poe. Have you spoken to him this morning?"

Abi's gaze narrowed. "I haven't seen him this morning. Did you check his room?"

"I did. He doesn't appear to be down here either." Now she was getting worried. Her nerves jangled. Poe wouldn't just try to leave without telling her. Her worry turned to suspicion, and she had a bad feeling that Abi knew more than he was telling.

"All right. Let's have a look," he suggested. "We can cover more ground if we split up. I'll go outside. You go through the house again."

She shook her head. "No. You go through the house.

I want to look outside." She'd already been through the house.

He started to argue but then decided against it. "Fine. Just keep a low profile. There are neighbors up here."

Jamie walked to the front door, pulled on her coat and headed outside. Excalibur Court was a single, dead end street. There were about a dozen large houses that circled the short street. The ones on their side overlooked the valley below where Dr. Case's house sat nestled amid the thick woods. On the other side of the street, the houses backed up to another cul-de-sac. The area was thickly wooded so there was some amount of privacy despite the number of houses.

Jamie walked to the end of the drive and surveyed the cul-de-sac. There were no vehicles in the driveways. There were probably rules about leaving a vehicle outside the garage. There was one dark sedan at the end of the cul-de-sac parked in the common area. She watched it for a moment. Didn't see anyone inside. The street was quiet. A breeze whipped through the air, reminding Jamie that it was almost Christmas and cold. Lots colder than in LA.

She liked the Los Angeles area, particularly the weather, but she spent most of her time in DC. Went with the territory of her work. She never knew where her next assignment would be. So far in the past year she had been assigned in all directions. Poe had worked with her on three missions.

Worry niggled at her again.

Where the hell was he?

She called his cell. Three rings and it went to voice mail. "Hey, where are you?"

A deeper worry started to gnaw at her. He wouldn't just leave like this. Not possible.

She walked around the yard. Ventured several yards into

the woods at the back of the house. No sign of Poe. She called out his name a couple of times with no response. This was wrong. Then she went back in the house.

Abi was on his phone.

Maybe Poe had called him with an explanation? But why wouldn't he call Jamie?

She kept her cool until Abi ended his call. Then she demanded, "Was that him?"

"No. It was not. In fact, that was a colleague who is monitoring the comings and goings on the roads in and out of this development and he says no one has come in or gone out this morning."

She wasn't surprised that he had backup watching the street. He would be a fool not to have support nearby. It would be nice if he shared details like that, but arguing about it right now wasn't an option.

"Something's wrong." Jamie moved to the wall of glass doors that led out onto the patio and looked out over the valley below. "He wouldn't just leave."

Abi joined her. "Are you sure about that?"

She turned on him. "What I'm sure about," she said pointedly, "is that if he isn't here, then something has happened to him and since you're in charge of this operation, it's your job to know what that is."

He moved his head side to side in a somber manner. "I have not seen him this morning."

"Then I suggest you back up the footage on your security cameras and see what happened." If he dared to tell her there were no cameras, she might just have to punch him.

He nodded. "I can do that."

In the living room, he picked up the remote to the television and turned it on. Then he opened a drawer on one of the side tables and withdrew another remote. This one he pointed at the television screen and made a number of selections.

A new app opened, and several views of the house appeared on the screen. He ran the video back and, sure enough, just before daylight, Poe exited a side door in the kitchen.

"You didn't set the alarm?" This was ridiculous. Why would Abi take that sort of risk?

"I did set the alarm before I went to bed. I can only assume he disarmed it. It was armed when I got up this morning, which is why I didn't consider that he'd gone outside."

Poe was good. Figuring out a way around the code to disarm the security system wasn't outside his purview, but why would he do that without telling her?

"The question," Abi went on, "is why would he leave?"

"It would not be because he wanted to," Jamie argued. If Abi was accusing Poe of something he could just back off. Poe would never double-cross her. She gestured to the screen. "Are there exterior cameras?" It was a silly question. Who had such an elaborate security system inside and then nothing outside?

Another click of the remote and they were looking at the yard around the house. The front was clear. So was the back. The view extended to the woods. While she watched, Abi ran the video back until it showed Poe as he walked out that side door.

Jamie held her breath as she watched him walk around the iron fence that separated the pool area from the rest of the yard. He continued past this area and straight toward the woods.

"This is wrong," Jamie said, outright fear rising inside her now.

"We should go out there and have a look," Abi suggested. He led the way to the same kitchen side door that Poe had used. They exited the house and walked the cobble-stone path toward the grassy area between the pool and the woods.

There was no way Poe would leave like this without telling her. *No way.* There had to be something about this that she didn't know. A call from someone who had warned of imminent danger. Something.

Once they were in the woods, the lack of light made seeing any disturbance of the underbrush difficult. Jamie stood still and visually searched the area, looking for any indication that a person had cut through that underbrush.

Then she saw what she was looking for. A bent twig on a limb. She headed in that direction. Abi was right behind her. She inspected the bushes and the ground. Someone had definitely been through here recently.

She turned on the flashlight app of her phone and scanned the ground. The light flashed over something shiny.

Her heart bumped harder against her sternum.

She reached down and sifted through the leaves. Her fingers hit a cool and firm object.

Her gut clenched as her fingers curled around a cell phone.

The screen of Poe's cell instantly lit with the missed call notifications from her attempts to reach him.

She started forward, looking for more indications of where the brush had been parted. Her heart pounded so hard she couldn't catch her breath. Why would he come out here? Why wouldn't he tell her whatever was on his mind?

A thought occurred to her, and she whirled on Abi. "You didn't plant any tracking devices?"

He looked away before answering the question. "Only on you. I wasn't expecting you to have company."

Fury roaring through her, she started to search once more. If Poe was lying out here injured, she needed to find him.

Abi didn't argue or question her actions. He just followed suit, picking his way through the brush and searching the same as she did.

An hour later it was obvious they weren't going to find him.

The underbrush became spotty as they neared the drop down the hillside. At that point there was no longer any indication Poe had been out there.

They went back in the house and watched the security footage. Poe went into the woods, but he never came out.

This was wrong, wrong, wrong.

Jamie paced the floor. Where would he have gone? She supposed he could have cut left and come out around one of the other houses.

"I need to check with the neighbors." That was the only possible next move.

"You can't do that," Abi argued. "We cannot call attention to ourselves."

"I don't care. I need to find my partner—my friend."

Abi held up his hands. "What you need is coffee."

Had he lost his mind? "I don't need coffee."

He poured a cup and placed it on the island. "Just sit down and drink. We need to think."

She took a breath and then did as he asked. She slid onto a stool and picked up the cup. She hadn't had any coffee this morning and suddenly she needed the caffeine desperately.

"First," Abi suggested, "let's approach this logically."

She drank from the cup rather than taking a bite out of his head.

"Let's consider the reasons Poe would leave." He gestured to her. "You know him better than me. What do you think?"

"Someone may have called him with information he couldn't ignore."

"Do you have the pass code for his phone so we can see who he has spoken to?"

She made a face. "If I did I would have already checked. All I saw were the latest notifications and that was where I called him. To see beyond that I would need the pass code."

"We can assume someone may have called him not only with news he couldn't ignore, but also with something he didn't feel he could share. Does he have family who may have needed his help?"

Jamie shook her head. "No one he's close to."

"What about your employer?"

"Maybe. But I can't imagine why he wouldn't have told me." That was the part that made no sense at all. Poe would not just leave like this...not while leaving her behind.

"Then we have to assume it's someone from this end."

She was surprised that Abi made the statement. "Is there someone who wanted to stop this mission? Maybe someone who feels it's the wrong move?"

"That's always possible, but I was not informed of this if that is the case. I can make some calls. See if there's something I should know. Check with my people to see if he's left the area."

Why the hell didn't he just say that already?

"I would appreciate that." She took a breath, forced her nerves to calm. "He wouldn't leave like this without telling me unless he felt there was no other option."

"Drink your coffee," Abi said again. "I'll make some calls."

He walked outside onto the patio. Jamie watched and

finished off her coffee. There was a chance Poe could have decided to take a risk to put protective measures in place. Not that she was going to share this with Abi. Poe didn't trust Abi. He was concerned about how this would shake down and, in Jamie's opinion, there was reason to be concerned. Poe may have believed that the best way to head off trouble was for him to bow out, making it look as if it was not voluntary. Then he would take up a position to watch, to be in place in the event Jamie needed an extraction.

It was an option they always discussed for their joint missions. It wasn't one they'd ever had to use. More important, they had not talked about the option in this situation.

Whatever the case, the fact that he didn't share his decision with her may have been to allow her to look completely uninvolved to Abi.

If that wasn't the case, then something bad had happened to Poe and Jamie was really worried. The possibility that Abi could be involved was all the more troubling.

If he was injured—or worse—and someone wanted answers about what they were doing, Poe was in serious trouble because he had no real answers. Until now, Abi had shared basically nothing with them beyond the name of the target.

Which, she supposed, was the point. You couldn't tell anyone what you didn't know.

For Poe, that could end up being a very bad thing. Not having the answers his abductor wanted wouldn't keep him alive.

Chapter Eight

2:00 p.m.

Kenny struggled to stay put as he watched Jamie take a walk around the cul-de-sac. She was still looking for him. She'd come outside and looked around several times. The worry and despair on her face cut straight through him.

He hated, hated, hated doing this to her, but it was necessary. It was the only way to provide any possible protection for her in the hours to come. He didn't blame Jamie for doing what she had to do. Her brother was being held hostage. She had no choice but to go along with what Amar wanted.

On some level, Jamie considered him a friend and Kenny couldn't say that he was an enemy, but what he could say was that the man was for sale to the highest bidder, which made him something worse than an enemy in Kenny's opinion. At least you knew the ultimate intentions of your enemy. There was no way to know for sure about a man like Amar. Where was he going with this? What did he expect to happen when all was said and done?

This was the trouble for Kenny.

Amar would do whatever necessary to accomplish his mission.

Kenny was not going to give him free rein to do as he

pleased. There had to be options for egress if the mission went to hell. Since Amar refused to share the details, Kenny had no choice but to intervene. Jamie was far too personally involved to fully trust her instincts.

He'd awakened early this morning and made the decision. He had to do something. Couldn't just wait. Waiting too long never proved to be the right strategy.

Jamie had no idea, but Victoria Colby-Camp had given him a burner phone to use for contacting her. He had not used it inside the house because he couldn't be sure what sort of monitoring Amar had going. The man was well prepared. Instead, Kenny had taken a walk around the cul-de-sac, much like Jamie was now, and made the calls. Victoria knew where they were, and she knew the identity of the target.

When he'd shared his concerns with Victoria, she had agreed that he had to make a move. With her blessing, he felt certain his decision had been the right one. Even Victoria felt Jamie wasn't thinking clearly. She was too worried about her brother. She was following orders toward that end. She would not be happy that he had voiced the concern to her grandmother, but he hoped it would prove the right move in the end.

Kenny watched Jamie walk back toward the house. The one he had chosen as his hideout was empty. The only unoccupied one in the cul-de-sac. The owners appeared to be on vacation. Perhaps visiting with family for the holidays.

The burner vibrated and he answered. "Hello."

"Kenny, we have some updated information."

Victoria and her team had been working to put together a list of potential patients suffering with inoperable brain tumors who possessed the means to put together an operation such as this one.

"I'm listening."

"We have a list of five patients in the state of Tennessee who have the means to take on an operation of this scale. We've put an investigator in place near the residence of each. Beyond that, we have another half dozen across the southeast who fit the same profile. I'm leaning toward the patient perpetrator as being local. Someone who would know Dr. Case's reputation well. Someone who had been exposed repeatedly to the headline-making leaps Case had taken in the field of neurosurgery."

"Sounds like you have the situation covered as well as anyone could." Good news in Kenny's opinion. "I've seen Jamie walking the cul-de-sac. She's still looking for me. She appears to be fine. Visibly worried, of course."

"I'm certain she's concerned," Victoria agreed.

"I'm uncomfortable misleading her this way," he admitted, "but it feels necessary. I'm trusting she'll understand that if I'm making a move like this, it's for the best."

He was good on that part, no matter that it felt wrong.

"Thank you for letting me know that you've had eyes on her. I've sent Ian Michaels to your location. He'll take a position the next street over. He has a vehicle for you if you need one." She confirmed the house number where Michaels would be waiting.

"Excellent." Kenny felt some sense of relief at the news. "I plan to try and keep eyes on Jamie, but I have no idea how they plan to get to the house where the party will take place. Amar claims to have invitations for tonight's party, but he could be lying."

"Lucas has done some careful research into Abidan Amar. His reputation is not quite as terrifying as I had feared, but he has a history of playing fast and loose with risk. I don't want him doing this with the lives of my grand-children."

Kenny could imagine Amar doing exactly that. What he couldn't see was Jamie or Luke as "grandchildren." But he understood and the idea made him smile. "The security system he has in place won't allow me to get close to the house again, but I left the bug you provided in the main living space. Hopefully, I'll hear the plan when he finally reveals the details to Jamie. Otherwise, I won't take my eyes off the place and when they move, I'll move."

"Keep me posted," Victoria urged. "We are prepared to do whatever necessary to help."

Sadly what they could do was limited. Any mistake could cost the life of the youngest Colby. They had no idea where Luke was or who was holding him. Outside interference could set off a deadly chain reaction.

"I will," Kenny assured her. "Thank you, Victoria."

He ended the call and considered that for months he had heard Jamie talk about her grandparents. He had done some deep research and despite how nice and normal they seemed, Jamie hadn't exaggerated one little bit. The Colby Agency was unlike any other agency of its kind. Victoria and her husband, Lucas, were legends, as were most of the investigators. If Kenny were in trouble, he would definitely want the Colby Agency on his team.

Frankly, he hoped to get to know them better in the future. He hoped to get to know Jamie a lot better as well. There were moments between them that made him believe the idea was possible. Either way, their friendship was invaluable, and he would do whatever necessary to protect that relationship.

Amar's voice sounded and Kenny turned to move closer to the speaker of the receiver.

Amar had apparently gotten a phone call.

His responses gave Kenny basically no information. Hopefully he would relate the update to Jamie when the call ended.

Whatever was going down was scheduled to do so tonight. Kenny needed to be prepared to intervene if necessary. To provide backup for Jamie either way. Listening and watching until there was a move was the only way for him to actually have her back. Had he stayed at the house, Amar would have made all the decisions and Kenny would have had no choice but to follow his orders. Amar would have possessed all the power.

This was the right move—as difficult as it had been to walk away from that house knowing he was leaving Jamie behind. The decision gave him some leeway to move as he saw fit.

The conversation between Amar and his caller appeared to be coming to an end.

Kenny held his breath. He couldn't afford to miss a word.

"Was that your point of contact?" Jamie asked.

"It was."

Kenny hoped the man intended to provide more detail than those two words.

"Do we have some change or addition to the mission?" Jamie prompted.

"Nothing I need to share at this time."

Her sigh was audible. "Really, you're going to stick to that worn-out line? Why even bother to involve me in this if you're going to keep me in the dark?"

"I have my orders, Jamie. When I can tell you more, I will. Every step of this operation is a strictly need-to-know basis only. You're familiar with how this works. I know you are. Let's not get bent out of shape with the rules."

"When you decide to stop playing games, let me know."

The sound of her walking out of the room wasn't what Kenny had hoped for. Maybe she was bluffing in an attempt to prod him into talking.

Then again, he had to admit that hearing her tell him off like that gave him a little kick of satisfaction.

As satisfying on a personal level as the exchange was, the real question was, how long did the guy intend to keep the details from her?

This was not the proper way to run an operation.

Chapter Nine

2:30 p.m.

"Jamie, wait!"

She hesitated at the bottom of the stairs. She was over his secretiveness. If they were in this together, he needed to tell her what the hell was going on. Good grief, they were only hours from when this thing was supposed to go down.

And Poe, damn it, was nowhere to be found.

She took a breath and turned to face Abi. "This thing is scheduled to go down tonight and you're still keeping me in the dark. Why am I even here?" She braced her hands on her hips. "You apparently intend to do this entirely alone. What am I? Arm candy?"

He laughed softly, then looked away. "You surely could be, but we won't go there." He blew out a breath then. Obviously not looking forward to coming out with it.

She braced her hands on her hips, out of patience. "Are we in this together or not?"

"There's been a slight change," he said. "Nothing to worry about. Originally, we were scheduled to arrive at eight tonight but now we're to be there at seven-thirty. I'm not pleased with the sudden change, but I can only assume some other sort of intelligence became available, prompting this schedule change."

The fact that he was genuinely upset seemed to suggest he was telling the truth. Either way, she was over this whole cloak and dagger game. They were on the same side after all.

"I need you to walk me through what's going to happen tonight. This beating around the bush has gone on long enough."

"All right. Let's sit down and I'll walk you through it."

It was about time. She followed him back to the living room area. He went to the bar and grabbed a couple of bottles of water and passed one to her. If not for that sudden phone call, she would be convinced his decision to share had something to do with Poe's absence. She hoped that was not the case.

"We will arrive at the party like any other guests. I've seen the list of invitees, and none are familiar to me. I'm assuming I will not be familiar to any of them. Same goes for you. Which is part of the beauty of the situation."

"Is there some aspect of his private residence that has been deemed more accessible than, say, the hospital or his clinic?" The private residence of a man such as Dr. Case likely included serious security services and a well-trained security team.

"The hospital where his surgery privileges are has state-of-the-art facial recognition for everyone going in and coming out," Abi explained. "It wouldn't prevent us from coming in, but it would not forget our faces. I'm sure neither of us wants that to happen."

"A good reason to rule out that location," she admitted. A hospital with facial recognition technology. Wow.

"His clinic is not equipped with technology quite so advanced, but the location creates a difficult exit strategy. Too congested...too many cameras on the surrounding buildings."

"I suppose the fact that the clinic operates only during regular business hours, daylight hours, creates a problem of its own."

"The cover of darkness is always an ally," he agreed.

"I'm sure there will be security cameras at the doctor's residence." Really, she was confident this was the case.

"You're right, but we have access to the system so no issues there."

Of course they did. Abi was too good to move forward without that key piece of intelligence.

"There will be some sort of precipitous event," she suggested. "A distraction?"

"A power outage. It's not so unique, but it will work and it's not so unusual this time of year."

"You have the layout of the residence?" Familiarizing herself with the floor plan would be useful. As for the power outage, that was always a workable strategy. Power outages happened—as he said, particularly during extreme temperatures. Living this far outside the city proper was asking for additional issues when it came to utilities.

"I do." He pulled out his cell and opened an image. "We enter via the front as one would expect."

The front door appeared to open into a large entry hall. He moved on to another image that showed a photo of the entry hall.

"Security will be here confirming that all who enter are on the list. From there we'll follow the others into the grand hall."

The grand hall was an area that branched off into a living room, dining room, library and—well beyond all that—a kitchen. Any one of those rooms was larger than the entire first floor of this house. The grand hall worked like a massive hub connecting all the other rooms. It made for the perfect area to linger in groups without interrupting the flow of those filtering into and through the other rooms.

"Once we're in," he went on, "we'll mingle, have hors d'oeuvres and a nonalcoholic drink. Just to blend in."

"Where is our egress?"

He slid the photo left, moving to another image. "Our priority exit is through the kitchen. We have two secondary options. Through the French doors in the library and off the back terrace outside the main living area."

"What's the layout for transportation around the property?" She'd looked at the house and property via the telescope, but some aspects were blocked from view by landscaping and other obstacles.

"We'll have two options for leaving. A helicopter from the doctor's helipad. This would give us a sort of emergency style departure. The hope would be that other guests assume there has been an emergency and the doctor had to go. The other option is via a limo that will be standing by in the front roundabout."

So far she had no complaints.

"What method of inducement do you plan to use to ensure his cooperation?" This was the part that concerned Jamie the most. She hoped he didn't intend to use drugs or physical coercion. Despite her reservations with either of those avenues, the problem was, there weren't that many other options. At least none she liked any better.

"We have that covered," he said as he closed his phone and slipped it into his hip pocket.

"Meaning?" she pressed. "Are we going in armed? Will he be drugged?"

"No drugs. No weapons."

She and Poe had discussed the possibility that the man's child would be used to gain his cooperation. "Then we're using the kid." Dread congealed in her gut. She hated the idea. Hated it even more than the drugs or weapons.

"You have my word," he said, his gaze pressing hers, "if it becomes necessary to use the child, she will not be harmed in any way."

Damn it. She knew it! "You can't make that promise. Things go wrong. Accidents. Mistakes. You can never predict how people will react to these situations."

Abi held up his hands as if to quiet her, which made her all the angrier. "This will happen quickly. In an orderly manner. There will not be time for mistakes or accidents."

People always thought a simple plan would go easy— no glitches. But there was no simple plan when it came to abducting another human. Not unless you rendered them unconscious.

The plan sounded perfect. Well thought out. Concise. Except all of that would go out the window when Dr. Case or his wife understood what was happening. If a guest happened to overhear…it would all go to hell in a heartbeat.

"You can't be sure of anything. Not one single thing that involves another human."

"You can't be sure I'm wrong."

She wasn't going to argue the point with him. Moving on, she said, "You've mentioned that we have a very narrow window of opportunity. Why is that the case? It's a party with guests who will be coming and going. Is there some sort of step or arrival—maybe a departure—that will happen that somehow renders our plans unusable? Is something turning into a pumpkin at a certain time?"

He didn't answer right away. And he didn't laugh. Mostly he stared at her, obviously attempting to decide how to answer.

He was just as worried as she was, but he would die before he would admit as much.

"It's the kid, isn't it?" Jamie shook her head. He might as well just spit it out. "It has to happen before she's tucked in for the night."

"Something like that," he confessed.

"I'm not good with this." But what could she do? Her brother's life was on the line. "If anything goes wrong—"

"I will not allow the child to be hurt," he insisted. "Really, you have my word on that."

She didn't doubt he meant what he said, but he could not guarantee the child's safety or the doctor's cooperation. He could only deduce the outcome based on common human behavior. The odds might lean slightly in his favor but there were no guarantees.

"What happens if the doctor is injured?" Had his employer thought of that? What they were about to do posed significant risk to all involved. "Then no one will have the benefit of the lifesaving surgery only he can do at this time."

"We can talk about what-ifs all night," Abi said. "But it's our job to make sure the what-ifs don't happen. We get the doc and his daughter out with no hitches. We do what we have to do and everybody's happy when the night is over."

Jamie held up her hands in surrender. Further discussion was pointless. "Moving on, please. At this point, I need some sort of assurance from you that your employer had nothing to do with Poe's disappearance." The facts were troubling. She had not heard from him, and his cell had ended up on the ground in the woods behind the house. If he'd been taken by someone involved in all this, why hadn't they heard anything? If he'd decided some other action was necessary, why hadn't she heard from him by now?

"I have no idea why or how he left other than what we found on the security system." Abi shrugged. "He told me nothing. I saw and heard nothing."

"You don't receive any sort of notification when someone enters or exits the house?"

"This is not my house. I'm a guest here just as you are. I had no reason to want to monitor who went in and out. It was only relevant if we were here and frankly, I wasn't expecting you or Poe to cut out on me."

"He wouldn't cut out without a reason," she said to ensure Abi understood this wasn't Poe just cutting out.

"You want to know what I think?" He braced his hands on the island. "I think he decided he didn't need to be part of this."

Jamie shook her head. "No way. He wouldn't do that. He would never leave me in the lurch."

Abi shrugged. "Maybe I'm wrong. I guess we'll find out tonight. If he shows up and tries to interfere, we'll have our answer. If he doesn't show up, we'll have an answer as well."

Jamie shook her head again. "You'll see." She wasn't standing around here and throwing her friend under the bus. She knew Poe too well. He had either set out on a plan of his own because he knew something was rotten with this one or someone had taken him. End of story.

She thought of his cell phone and worry dug deep beneath her skin. She desperately hoped her allowing Poe to come here with her wasn't going to be the reason he…

No. She wasn't going there.

"Let me know when you're ready to move." Jamie needed a few minutes to herself. Some time to decompress and get her head on straight. Tonight, was far too important to go into it rattled like this. Psyching herself up for a mission was always a smart step.

Abi touched her arm to slow her departure. "I'm counting on you, Jamie. I can't do this without you."

"Yeah."

Jamie had never felt so torn. This was not like her usual missions. It was wrong. More wrong than anything she'd ever been asked to do. But it was also the only way to save her brother.

She couldn't say no...couldn't walk away.

And because of that she had no choice but to do all within her power to ensure that Dr. Case and his daughter cooperated—but also that they survived this thing unscathed.

For the first time since she was a little girl, she wished her grandmother were here beside her to give her an assist. She could use some of Victoria's wisdom and strength right now.

Lionheart Court,
7:30 p.m.

JAMIE EMERGED FROM the limo that had picked up her and Abi. He waited for her outside the car, looking too handsome in his black suit and black bow tie against the white shirt. His dark skin and black hair gave him the sophisticated look of a foreign diplomat. In his jacket pocket was a red handkerchief.

Her floor length sheath was the exact shade of red as the handkerchief. So were her very sleek high heeled shoes. None of which was made for running or for tackling an enemy.

After seeing the formfitting dress, she'd decided to wear

her hair up in a French twist. Seemed appropriate. Whatever others thought of them being at this party, they certainly made a handsome couple. Jamie felt as if she'd arrived at senior prom with the most popular boy in school, but couldn't remember why she'd decided to come when none of her friends would be here. Only this boy who was so handsome and far too charming.

There were always strangers involved with her missions, but these were not simply strangers. These were civilians who had no idea that this party had been targeted by someone who had so much money at his disposal that he could choose to disrupt this gala and the life of the man hosting it to get what he wanted.

Jamie took a breath and cleared her head. She knew what she had to do. Fretting over the details wouldn't get the job done.

Abi took her hand and draped it over his arm. "In case I haven't already told you, you look amazing."

She smiled at the man who held the door open as they entered the home of their target. "You look quite fetching yourself, Mr. Amar."

He flashed her a smile.

Once they were deep into the entry hall, he leaned close and whispered, "Do you think we look so nice that they'll never suspect we're here for nefarious purposes?"

"As long as they don't look too closely."

He smiled. "Touché."

Apparently, the doctor had many friends. The crowd was larger than Jamie had expected for a family holiday gathering.

They entered the grand hall, and it was like entering a Christmas wonderland. Beautifully decorated trees…garlands and ribbons…so tastefully done. The scent of cedar hung in the air. Holiday music played softly from speakers hidden somehow in the architecture. The ceiling towered two stories above, looking exactly like something from a European castle. The floor was marble and the furnishings were museum quality. Servers strolled about with their trays. But Jamie wasn't the slightest bit hungry or even thirsty.

"Recognize anyone?"

She had seen photos of Case and his family on the internet and on Abi's phone. Jamie spotted Dr. Case near the massive stone fireplace almost immediately. He was surrounded by what she presumed were colleagues. Maybe close friends. This didn't feel like a family holiday gathering. This was almost certainly a business function accented with holiday decor.

"Several other surgeons," he said, leaning close enough for her to feel his lips brush her forehead. "A number of local politicians."

Interesting. Abi had certainly familiarized himself with those in the doctor's orbit. Not surprising really, she decided. This was exactly what she did when prepping for a mission.

She spotted Case's wife. She too wore a red dress. Jamie glanced at Abi. "Am I wearing red because she is?"

He smiled. "It's a very good color on you. Far better than on her. And your blond hair is natural, unlike hers."

Hovering near Mrs. Case was her daughter. Ten-year-old Lillian Case. And of course, she wore a red dress to match her mommy. Oh, dear God. Jamie felt sick at what could go wrong.

"Do you have any assets here or nearby?" She gazed around at the lavish crowd. Some part of her hoped to spot Poe. Damn it. Where was he? "Someone to call upon for backup in case we need it?"

"No assets inside. Just the two of us."

At least he wasn't ruling out the possibility of backup somewhere on the property.

Better than nothing.

Jamie considered the most likely tactic for making this happen in a crowd of this size, in a house of this size.

"I'm guessing the family has a routine for their daughter. A certain time to go to bed. Mommy tucks her in, and Daddy pops by for a good-night kiss. Where's the nanny? Have you made arrangements for disabling her?"

"The nanny tucks her in. Then Mommy and Daddy go to the room for a quick good-night. It's all very affable and everyone disappears quickly. The nanny goes home after. But tonight the nanny is not an issue. She's on vacation for the next ten days."

One less potential liability.

"You know—" Jamie glanced around in search of a server "—I think I might need a real drink after all."

"Allow me," Abi said before making a slight bow and then hurrying to the nearest server.

Jamie watched Mrs. Case for a moment and then her husband, the doctor. She wondered if either could possibly comprehend how their lives were about to change. The ability to breathe suddenly felt unnatural, difficult.

This was wrong.

And yet she was helpless to stop it.

Abi reappeared with two flutes of bubbling liquid. Jamie accepted hers and took the smallest sip. "Thank you."

"Case's wife writes children's books."

Jamie nodded. "You mentioned that, and I spotted it on her Wikipedia page."

"Her latest is *The Fish in My Dreams*. It's about a little

girl who dreams of swimming deep into the ocean with fish on her feet instead of shoes."

Jamie laughed. "Sounds like something her daughter dreamed and told her about."

Abi nodded. "That's what she says in the dedication to her daughter."

Jamie slipped her arm around his. "I'm guessing we should tell her how much we loved the book."

"The daughter will remember you talking to her mother," he agreed.

The whole point.

Jamie led the way across the room. Mrs. Case looked up as they approached.

"Mrs. Case," Jamie said, her smile broadening, "I'm Jasmine Colter. I just wanted to say how very much my little niece enjoyed your new book."

Lillian leaned closer to her mom, her cheeks pink.

"It's Lillian's story really." She beamed down at her daughter. "She has very vivid dreams."

Jamie nodded to Lillian. "Such a great story, Lillian. I hope you'll be telling more stories with your mom."

Lillian smiled finally. "Ducks are coming next."

"Oh my. You're writing a story about ducks?"

Lillian nodded. "For next year."

"How wonderful. We'll be sure to get it."

They chatted for a moment more until another guest arrived to share her praise for the book. Jamie and Abi wandered to the other side of the room.

"We are twenty minutes out," he told her.

Jamie left her barely touched glass on a tray. "I think I'll drop by the powder room."

"I'll be right here." His position allowed him to see the wife, daughter and the doctor.

Jamie nodded and headed through the lingering crowd.

Taking a bathroom break while wearing a dress like this was never fun. But she might as well take advantage of the opportunity. No way to know when she'd have another chance. Ducking behind a bush wearing this wouldn't be so easy.

She made quick work of the necessary business. After a swift wash of her hands and check of her hair and makeup, she smoothed her dress. It was almost showtime. Maybe they would all get through this without a glitch, and she would be on her way home tomorrow with her little brother in tow.

"Hang in there, Luke." She hoped she would be seeing him soon.

She exited the ornate powder room and went in search of her date. Well, *date* wasn't really the right term. *Partner in crime.* No sign of the mother and daughter. She surveyed the room again. She spotted them by the larger Christmas tree. It was then that she noticed their dresses fit particularly well with the holiday decor. Every last thing was meticulously coordinated.

"They'll be going up soon," Abi told her. "When the doctor goes up, that will be our cue."

"Have you heard from your getaway driver? You've confirmed that all is as it should be?" Her nerves were jangling.

"I have. All is exactly as it should be."

"When and how will your employer release Luke?"

His gaze collided with hers. "Once Dr. Case is at the designated location, you will be taken to Luke's condo, and he will be there waiting for you."

"And when will the doctor be returned to his home?"

"By noon tomorrow I'm told."

She wondered if he would be considered missing or kidnapped during that time. If so the police and the FBI would launch into action. Or would he simply be made to call his wife and assure her that he'd had an emergency at the hospital?

"Until then," Abi said, drawing her back to the conversation, "he'll be caring for an emergency situation. It happens all the time. His wife and daughter will think nothing of it."

Jamie searched his face. He'd just lied to her, or he'd made the sort of mistake he shouldn't and he'd glossed right over it.

"Does he usually take his daughter with him to emergencies?"

Abi stared at her for a long moment. "Before the mother realizes she is missing, little Lillian will be back in her room."

"What will she tell her mother? Another dream for a book?"

Suddenly all the holes in his elaborate plan were far too visible and Jamie had a bad, bad feeling swelling in her gut.

He smiled. "Sounds like a bestseller."

As long as no one died or was gravely injured, she reminded herself. Jamie settled her gaze on the doctor. How did a man like him—who possessed a skill like no one else—get through each day knowing he could only save a few? How did he decide who he would save and who he would let go?

Did he have the typical god complex associated with some in the profession?

Even as she asked herself this question, his shoulders seem to visibly slump beneath the weight of his success.

Or maybe she wanted to believe he cared that much. After all, imagine the dedication and work required to reach the sort of skill level he possessed. To achieve what no one else had.

She would soon know how he saw himself. More important, how he saw the patients in need of his help.

She hoped for the sake of all involved that he would be reasonable...not that there was anything reasonable about what was coming.

Chapter Ten

8:40 p.m.

Mrs. Case motioned for her daughter who was admiring the many decadent looking desserts spread across silver trays. Or perhaps it was the chocolate fountain in the middle of that table that had her mesmerized.

Either way, Lillian turned away empty-handed and skipped toward her mother. Almost bedtime. Sweet treats were apparently off the menu.

Jamie wondered if it was Abi's appearance at the dessert table that had alerted the child's mother. He'd insisted on finding something chocolate.

If his sudden need for chocolate hadn't made Jamie suspicious, seeing Dr. Case withdraw his cell phone from his jacket pocket for the first time since their arrival certainly did. The doctor turned from the trio to whom he'd been engaged in conversation. The three continued with whatever discussion they'd been having but the doctor's posture changed dramatically as he listened to the more personal conversation.

Abi appeared next to her with a delicious looking offering. She shook her head. "Something's happening."

She'd no sooner said the words than Dr. Case ended his

call and moved back toward the trio he'd abandoned. She didn't need a listening device to get the gist of what he was saying. His body language spoke loudly and clearly as he patted one man's shoulder and gave nods to the others. He was excusing himself.

Next to her, Abi suddenly reached for his cell phone.

Jamie ignored his subdued murmuring. She was far more interested in what was happening with the doctor. He crossed to his wife and daughter, said a few words, then dropped a kiss on each of their cheeks.

He was leaving.

He hurried from the room. Jamie drifted toward the front of the great hall, then on to the entry hall just in time to watch him disappear through the front double doors with no less than four men dressed in black accompanying him. Members of his security team, no doubt.

When she turned back to find Abi, he was moving in her direction. He put his arm around her shoulder and leaned close to her temple. "There's an emergency at the hospital."

"Are we staying here to await his return or going to the hospital?" She smiled up at him as if they were sharing secret love messages.

"We go with the doctor."

A final glance at the wife and daughter showed the wife smiling with friends and the daughter having wrangled a dessert without her mother noticing. The other guests appeared unconcerned about the doctor's abrupt departure. The servers continued offering drinks and finger foods and the music played on.

Jamie followed Abi from the house. The night was colder than when they'd arrived or perhaps it was only because the anticipation-fueled adrenaline related to what could happen had worn off, reminding her she'd opted not to wear a coat.

Abi said nothing until they were in the car traveling away from the house. "You'll find a change of clothes in the back seat."

She'd expected there would be a change of clothes for them at their next destination, but she hadn't anticipated it being in the car. Turned out to be a good decision.

She tucked up her dress and slid somewhat awkwardly over the console into the back seat. A pair of jeans, a sweater and sneakers were folded neatly on the seat. When had he done this? She supposed he had not. More likely someone had prepared everything to his specifications.

Unzipping the dress wasn't exactly the easiest feat, but she managed. She eased the luxurious fabric down her hips and over her legs.

"You have everything under control back there?" He glanced in the rearview mirror.

"I do." She pulled the sweater over her head and tugged it into place. She kicked off the heels and slipped into the jeans. This was a relief. She'd always felt more at home in jeans than in anything else.

She folded the dress and placed it on the seat, then set the shoes atop it. A quick search of the floorboard using the flashlight app on her cell helped her find a pair of socks. When the socks and sneakers were on, she was set, except for her hair. Making quick work of the task, she removed the pins, shook her hair free and then did a quick braid. It was best if she didn't look anything like the blonde in the red dress from the party.

"Any idea on how this changes our plans?"

"We'll wait until—"

Jamie's gaze swung to the rearview mirror. She didn't have to ask why he'd suddenly stopped talking. The bright lights filling the mirror provided the answer.

They had a tail.

"Brace yourself." Abi's fingers visibly tightened on the steering wheel.

Rather than risk looking back, Jamie braced her feet against the back of the passenger seat and eased down low in her seat.

The crash of metal was followed by a hard lurch forward as the other car rammed them. A new wave of adrenaline rose inside her.

Abi righted their forward momentum. "There's a weapon under my seat if you can get to it."

Jamie eased down into the floorboard and felt around under the driver's seat. The weapon sat snugly in a holster that had been secured to the bottom of the seat. A bit of creativity was required to remove the weapon from behind since it had been installed with the driver in mind.

"Got it."

She eased up into the seat, keeping her head low.

"He's coming again," Abi warned.

Jamie got onto her knees facing the rear window and watched as the vehicle neared. It was impossible to determine if there were more occupants than the driver. She powered the window down and leaned out as far as she dared.

"He's coming," Abi warned.

Jamie closed one eye and focused on the front passenger side wheel barreling toward her. She took the shot.

Tires squealed as the car seemed to spin sideways and rush backward. In fact, it was only because they were going forward that the distance stretched out between them.

"Bravo!" Abi shouted.

The car rocketed forward as he pushed the accelerator for all it had to offer.

Jamie powered the window back up but kept her focus

on the disabled car. It was dark, black maybe, and it wasn't moving.

Once it was out of view, she climbed over the console and settled back into the front passenger seat. She placed the weapon on the console and secured her seat belt.

"Who could have known about your plan?"

He slowed for an upcoming traffic signal. "I don't think this was someone who had advance knowledge of our plan. I'm thinking this was more like security picking up on our interest in the doctor's departure from the party."

"You're suggesting they monitored the guests who left when or soon after the doctor did."

"I am." He made a left turn.

"Maybe."

"Either that or your friend Poe tried taking us out of the game."

Of course he would come up with that scenario. "No. Poe would have followed us and then confronted us at our destination."

"At least one of us has faith in his motives."

"Whoever that guy was, if he works for the doctor, he's going to notify security at the hospital. They'll be watching for us."

"No problem." He glanced at her. "I have a plan."

Two more turns and he pulled into a slot in a parking area between two other vehicles. When he'd shut off the lights and the engine, he shifted in his seat to face her. "There's a sweater back there for me and a pair of sneakers. It might be easier for you to reach them."

The two items were in the floorboard after the erratic driving. She released her seat belt, got on her knees in the seat and reached into the rear floorboard. She passed the sweater and then the sneakers to him. His grin told her he'd enjoyed seeing her in that awkward position. She rolled her eyes.

His jacket, shirt and bow tie flew over the seat. He tugged the sweater over his head and rolled it into place. He powered the seat back to facilitate changing his shoes.

His cell vibrated and he took the call. "Yes."

Jamie surveyed the area. A multistory building sported a Nashville Eye Center logo. The hospital that was their destination, Saint Thomas, stood across the street. On that side of the street there were steps leading up to the parking area, making their current position well camouflaged from anyone who might be watching for their arrival. *Good move.*

He put the phone away and turned to her. "A patient he operated on early this morning developed an issue, which is why he's been called back here. We're going to hang around and then follow him back to the house." He sent her a pointed look. "At a safe distance and in a different car, of course."

"Of course."

They exited the car and headed across the street. The wind whipped across her face, making her flinch. Despite knowing that Poe wasn't the one who had followed them, she couldn't help looking around. Where the hell was he? She glanced at Abi. If he was responsible for whatever had happened to Poe...

She wasn't prepared to go there just yet. There had to be another explanation. Poe would not abandon her under any circumstances. However, as she'd already considered, he very well might take a different tactic to help with whatever he feared was coming.

She had every intention of giving him the benefit of the doubt either way...until there was no longer room for doubt.

They didn't enter the hospital through the lobby. Instead, they used the garage entrance. It was open twenty-four hours a day and since they had not arrived at the garage in a vehicle, the chances that security had spotted them via the cameras was unlikely. The cameras were only at the entrance and exit. Crossing over a short concrete wall in an area well camouflaged by shrubs near the entrance had protected them from view. Then they took the stairs to the level where the sky bridge crossed over to the hospital. Too easy.

"You have some idea of where we're going?" Jamie asked as they moved along the corridor. So far no one had paid attention to their arrival.

"Surgery, I presume." He flashed a smile.

Maybe it was that hint of a British accent, but his answer grated on her nerves. Of course the doctor was here for a possible return to surgery but that didn't mean she and Abi would be hanging out there. The goal was not to be spotted by the doctor's security team.

Careful to avoid eye contact with anyone they passed, they wound through the hospital until they reached the entrance to the surgery center. From there it was necessary to fly under the radar. Visiting hours were over and the usual excuses for their presence were no longer available.

Three people were seated in the surgery center's waiting room. Jamie assumed they had friends or family who'd had to undergo emergency surgery. Then again, for all she knew, surgeries were scheduled all hours of the day and night.

"You wait here," Abi said. "I'll have a look around. See if there's a need for anything beyond just hanging around."

If this was a true emergency with a patient, they had nothing to worry about.

"Whatever you say." She walked into the waiting room and took a seat where she could watch the corridor through the glass wall. If any dudes in all black showed up, she was following.

Abi watched her for a moment before going on his way. She pulled out her cell and then put it back. She couldn't call Poe. His cell was back at the house, disabled. Damn it. She thought of the car that had followed them on the way here. Case's personal security couldn't have known they were at the house on Excalibur...could they?

Why would they? The doctor's personal security team wouldn't likely have gotten a heads-up on a potential kidnapping plan.

Would they?

Only if Abi's employer was very, very bad at keeping secrets.

Then again, it could be as Abi suggested and the follower had been a member of Case's team who'd followed them from the house to ensure they weren't trouble...except she wasn't buying the idea that they would go so far as to ramming a guest's car. Following it, she could see. After some time to mull it over, she was confident Abi had gotten that one wrong. Or simply gave her the story to cover the fact that he had no idea where the car had come from.

A man in scrubs and a surgical gown entered the waiting room and one of the two women who had already been present when Jamie arrived rushed toward him.

They spoke, heads together, for a moment, then the man patted her on the shoulder and left.

Standing in the middle of that waiting room, the woman lapsed into tears, her hands covering her face.

Since no one else moved to go to her, Jamie did. She grabbed the box of tissues on the table next to her chair and walked over to where the woman stood crying. "Are you all right?" Not exactly the most original conversation starter, but there it was.

The woman looked at her, eyes red and filled with tears. Jamie offered her the box of tissues.

She tugged a couple free. "Thank you."

"Would you like to sit down?" Jamie asked.

The woman blew her nose, dabbed at her eyes and then shook her head. "I'm fine. Really. I'm only crying because I'm so grateful."

She glanced around the room. The television was set to a news channel with the sound muted. The two anchors' words scrolled across the bottom of the screen.

"Do you mind if we step into the corridor?" She shivered. "It's really cold in here."

She was right. It was cold as hell in here. "Of course." Jamie followed her into the corridor. "You were saying you were grateful."

She sagged against the glass wall as if she could no longer hold her weight. "It was all just a mistake."

Since they were at a hospital—the surgery area of the hospital—a mistake wasn't necessarily something for which to be thankful.

"My husband had surgery this morning." Her face furrowed into a frown. "A brain tumor. We were so incredibly thankful when the surgery was a success. But then tonight the nurse insisted on calling the doctor back. She said my husband was having a possible bleed—a brain bleed."

Jamie made a horrified face. "Oh, that sounds terrifying."

"It was. The strangest thing was that he seemed fine. But after she told us this and gave him something in preparation for a second surgery, he had a seizure." She clasped her hands together against her chest as if in prayer. "I was certain I was losing him." Her lips trembled.

"But he's all right now?"

"It's the craziest thing. Dr. Case's assistant—" she made a face "—not assistant but resident or whatever he is. A doctor," she said, frustrated at herself, "who works with Dr. Case said that everything was fine. It was some sort of error."

So this was why Dr. Case had been called back to the hospital. A mistake. Jamie wondered how often something like that happened. "Do you recall the nurse's name?"

The other woman made a face and shook her head. "The resident or doctor asked me that as well. I believe it was Johnson. Brenda or Beverly Johnson." She flattened her hands to her chest. "My Lord, I have to call our daughter and my husband's sister. They're all waiting to hear. Fearing the worst, I'm sure."

"I'm certainly glad all is well, Mrs...? I'm sorry, I didn't get your name."

"Teresa Mason. My husband is Johnny." She smiled, her lips trembling. "And he's going to be fine. The doctor said so."

"That's wonderful. My name is Jamie, by the way. Can I walk you back to his room?" She mentally crossed her fingers. If this woman's husband was Dr. Case's patient, then Jamie was sticking close to her for as long as she could.

"That would be so kind of you. They said he would be back in the room very shortly. I want to be there when he arrives."

Jamie walked alongside the lady who rambled on and on about the two of them, she and her husband, having recently shared their fortieth anniversary.

"How did you hear about Dr. Case?" Jamie asked. "I understand it's tough to get on his schedule."

"Oh my, yes, it is. We were so very lucky in that he was on call when Johnny lost consciousness. We had no idea anything was wrong. Dr. Case is the only reason he survived that brain tumor. We had no idea it was even there."

Jamie was surprised that surgeons like Case were ever "on call." Then again, she wasn't that familiar with the way physicians' schedules worked and certainly she had no idea how much of their time was owed to or pledged to a particular hospital.

"The other doctor said Dr. Case would pop into the room once Johnny was settled."

Jamie would try her best to hang around until Case arrived. No reason to believe he would recognize her. Once they were in the room she should shoot a text to Abi. He might not be aware of the ruse that brought Case to the hospital.

In Jamie's opinion the whole thing screamed of a setup for when the doctor left the hospital. He would have only a few security guards with him. Far less backup than he had at his home.

She and Mrs. Mason had just entered the room when Mr. Mason was rolled through the door on a gurney that looked more like a bed. Since there wasn't a bed in the room, Jamie assumed it was not just a gurney.

"He'll be groggy for a while," a nurse explained as she and a colleague moved his bed in place. "And he may sleep off and on. But don't worry. We'll be watching him closely."

Mrs. Mason parked herself next to his bed and took her husband's hand in hers. "Thank you so much," she told the nurses. "I appreciate all you do."

Jamie wondered how many people bothered to express their gratitude in this way.

The nurses made their way out and another figure entered.

Dr. Case.

Jamie stayed put in the corner by the visitor's chair. She avoided direct eye contact. She felt confident he wouldn't recognize her, but why take the chance.

"Mrs. Mason, thankfully we did not have to go back in. As my associate told you, we determined that all was well. We'll take another CT scan in a couple of hours just to be sure. Once that's completed, I'll let you know those results as soon as we have them. But I'm confident you have nothing to worry about."

"Thank you so much, Dr. Case."

He gave her a nod, then looked to Jamie. "May I speak with you in the corridor?"

Holy cow. Was he speaking to her? Since he stared directly at her, she assumed so. Mrs. Mason was whispering softly to her husband.

Jamie mustered up a vague smile. "Sure."

Maybe he had recognized her.

Oh hell.

Once they were outside the room and the door closed, he set his attention on Jamie. "Were you here in the room when the nurse told Mrs. Mason I needed to be called?"

Aha. They were attempting to nail down the reason this happened. "No. I'm sorry. I wasn't here." At his frustrated look, she shrugged and offered, "I went for coffee."

"Anyway," Case said. "I'm here now and I'll be hanging around for a while. Just as a precaution."

Obviously, he was worried this Nurse Johnson had done something more than make a fake call. Damn.

"If you or Mrs. Mason notice anything unusual, don't hesitate to call for assistance."

"We will. Thank you."

Case walked away. By the weary set of his shoulders, he

seemed exhausted. His day had begun very early and certainly had not ended the way he had anticipated.

She decided to call Abi rather than bother with a text.

"Where are you? I'm in the waiting room."

She gave him the abridged version of what had occurred. "Doesn't sound like Case is going home anytime soon."

"I'll make some calls about this fake nurse."

"Dr. Case feels overly safe here at the hospital," she said, thinking about how he'd come to the room alone. "He didn't have any of his security personnel with him when he visited the patient's room. Considering what just went down with the nurse, I'm not so sure that's a good thing."

"That is a very astute observation, Colby," Abi said. "I'll have to ensure he's made aware of this oversight."

Jamie had no idea how he intended to make that happen.

"You want me to hang around here? Case said he would be stopping back by?"

"Yes, please do. I have something else to look into."

"I'll let you know when I see him again." She ended the call and put her phone away.

At the Mason's door, Jamie knocked softly and pushed the door inward far enough to step inside. "Mrs. Mason, Dr. Case will be back after the next CT is taken. Do you need anything for now? My friend is still in surgery, so I have some time if you need anything."

"You are so kind. I'm good for now though."

"Great." Jamie frowned. "They seem a bit concerned about this Nurse Johnson."

Mason made a distressed face. "It's so strange. It makes me wonder if she was even a nurse or if she was high or something."

Jamie wondered the same thing. "What did she look like?"

"Brown hair. Short and spiky." She scrunched her face

in thought. "Kind of tall." She shrugged. "I always think anyone taller than me is tall. But a couple or three inches taller than me for sure. Thin. Kind of willowy."

"I'm sure they'll get to the bottom of it," Jamie assured her. "They have cameras everywhere here. Maybe she was from one of those temp agencies." Jamie shrugged. "There are so many staffing shortages these days."

If the point of this nurse's lie about Mr. Mason was to get Dr. Case back to the hospital, why would she just disappear without completing the rest of her mission? Had her backup failed to step up? Or had the plan not been executed as of yet?

Which meant Dr. Case could be in danger right now.

"I think I'll take a walk," Jamie said. "You sure I can't get you anything?"

Mason shook her head. "No, thank you." She exhaled a big breath. "I really appreciate your help tonight. You were so very kind."

"You're very welcome, but it was nothing. Just being a good human."

As soon as she was in the corridor, she called Abi again. "I think we might still have a problem."

"I was thinking the same thing," he said, sounding breathless. "Case is in the doctor's lounge. I'm close by. Two members of his security team are stationed at the door. So far no word on who this nurse is or who is behind whatever went down or is going down."

"Then we're not going anywhere until he does."

"You got it. We need to know where he is every moment until we make *our* move."

Hopefully someone else wasn't going to beat them to the next move.

Chapter Eleven

Chicago
Colby Residence,
11:00 p.m.

Victoria opened a box of ornaments she'd had for at least thirty years, maybe forty. How time flew. There were dozens of boxes of decorations and here she was trying to pull this all together at nearly midnight. But she certainly couldn't sleep.

She stared at the tree. On the way home last evening she'd insisted that Lucas stop at the pop-up Christmas store on the corner and pick out something lovely. They'd thought they wouldn't bother with a tree this year since no one would be home for the holidays anyway and the two of them were set to go to Paris.

But she wasn't sure she could go. Not until she knew for certain that Jamie and Luke were safe. She suspected Lucas had picked up on her hesitation, which was why he didn't question her request for a tree.

She picked up a glossy green ornament. How could she leave with all this uncertainty hanging around them like a dark cloud? Tasha's situation remained unknown. Luke was missing. Jamie had been forced to throw in with a man Victoria did not trust to find her brother.

"You should come to bed, dear."

She looked up as Lucas entered the room. He wore those favorite pajamas of his. She smiled. The blue ones that made his gray eyes look so bright. She loved those pajamas too. She loved him. So very much.

"I thought I'd hang a few ornaments." She draped the green ornament on a branch. The smell of cedar had filled the house and she so loved it. How foolish she had been to even consider not putting up a tree.

It was a tradition. She and Lucas always had a tree.

Lucas joined her and picked out a blue ornament from the box. "I love these ornaments."

They were plain. No glitter or painted flowers or other symbols of Christmas. But there were literally hundreds of them. Red ones, pink ones. Silver, gold, blue and green. Even a few white ones. By the time the branches were loaded with ornaments, they would be beautiful.

"Wait. Wait." Lucas held up a hand. "We have to put the lights on first."

How had she forgotten the lights? "That was always your job," she said, not wanting anything to do with that chore. "I'll make hot chocolate if you string the lights."

He gave her a look that suggested he wasn't quite sure that was a fair trade, then he smiled. "Hot chocolate sounds lovely. Perhaps you'll add a little rum to mine."

"Mine too," she agreed.

Victoria padded into the kitchen. She set a pan on the stove and added the milk, then turned on the flame. While the milk heated, she combined the chocolate and sugar and added it to mugs. Hot chocolate was a winter favorite around here. If it snowed, they had hot chocolate. She glanced out the window over the sink. The snow was still coming down. The weather forecast predicted it would snow all night.

It was beautiful and a little heartbreaking. It would be the perfect time to have everyone together. But that wasn't going to happen.

This would be the first time they'd been spread so far and wide at Christmas. Victoria couldn't help feeling a little nostalgic and a lot sad.

Her cell vibrated in the pocket of her robe. Her heart rate sped up as she pulled it free of the silk. It was Kenny. "Kenny, do you have news?"

"I'm at the Saint Thomas Hospital in Nashville."

Victoria's heart dropped into her stomach. "Is everyone all right?" Please, please let her grandchildren be safe.

"Yes. Jamie is here. I've seen her. She and Amar followed the doctor from his house to the hospital. But I was careful that neither she nor Amar saw me."

"Was going to the hospital part of the plan?"

"No, ma'am. Whatever happened, it was some sort of emergency. The doctor left the party and Jamie and Amar followed not far behind. There was a small incident en route with someone who was following them. I've sent the license plate information to Michaels in hopes we might learn who it was."

More thumping in her chest. "What sort of incident?"

"The unidentified driver attempted to run them off the road. He might be someone who works for the doctor and who thought their following him from the party was suspicious, but I'm leaning more in the direction of another outside source."

Dread congealed in Victoria's belly. "Someone else who wants to, perhaps, kidnap the doctor."

"I fear so," he said. "I'm also concerned as to how this stacks up based on what you've learned about Dr. Case."

The additional intelligence her people had collected certainly shed a bad light on Dr. Case, but there were always two sides to every story. At this point it was best to reserve judgment.

"Very well," Victoria said, the next step clearing in her mind. "Given what we know, I believe it's time for you to return to the team."

"I agree. At this point I feel too removed from what's happening to be useful."

"Call me as soon as you've made contact with Jamie again."

"Will do. Good night, Victoria."

The call ended and she said a quick prayer for Jamie and Luke as well as Kenny and Amar. The smell of scorching milk shook her from the worrisome thoughts.

"You need some help in there?"

She shook off the troubling thoughts and emptied the milk, then started over. "Just giving you plenty of time to string those lights."

"Ha ha!" he called back to her.

She looked out the window and this time she couldn't help smiling. Why was she so worried about Jamie and Luke? They were Colbys. They would get through this and complete the mission too.

It was the Colby way.

Monday, December 24

One Day Before Christmas

Chapter Twelve

4:00 a.m.

"Your people have no idea who set this event in motion?" Jamie was having a difficult time getting past the notion that Abi and his backers had no idea how this *mistake* went down.

He kept his focus on the dark highway as they drove back toward the Case home. The doctor and his entourage were half a mile ahead. Abi had carefully kept his distance since leaving the parking area at the hospital.

"If my people have intel on last night, they're not sharing the information with me." He glanced at her through the darkness. "Frankly, unless there's a reason for me to know, I actually do not care to hear about it."

Now that was a cop-out. "Please. Do not try to spin this for me. Remember who you're talking to, friend. This is not my first rodeo."

The entourage up ahead took the turn to Lionheart Court.

Abi slowed, giving them ample time to move farther along the private drive leading to the doctor's home before they reached the intersection.

He blew out a long, low whistle as they passed that exit. "At least we know he made it home without being whisked away by a competitor."

Jamie waited until Abi had blown past the turn the doctor and his team had taken and then took the next right on Lady of the Lake Lane, which would take them to Excalibur. Following the doctor hadn't been an option. They had been at the hospital keeping an eye on the situation for hours. Case hadn't wanted to leave until he was certain all was good with Mr. Mason.

Jamie hoped the patient's continued stability meant he was out of the woods for good. Mason and his family would certainly have a lot to celebrate this Christmas. To find yourself on death's door and then suddenly pulled back by the skill of a surgeon was the very definition of a miracle.

Abi pulled into the garage of the Excalibur house, and she wondered again where Poe was and what in the world he was doing. If he had come here to help her and he'd ended up in trouble, she would never forgive herself.

She should call her grandmother to see if she had heard from him. Though she couldn't see Poe calling Victoria and not calling her, there could be a reason she didn't understand. She got out of the car and reached back inside for the dress and shoes she had worn to the party. Abi tucked his weapon in his waistband and grabbed his discarded clothes as well. There were things she wanted to say, but right now, she wanted a long, hot shower and a couple hours of sleep.

She wasn't sure either would happen, but she could hope.

Abi reached for the door of the house and stalled. He instantly reached to his waistband and the weapon he had tucked there not ten seconds ago as he got out of the vehicle.

He jerked his head toward her and she stepped to the side of the door. Abi held the weapon ready and eased in through the door that Jamie could now see stood ajar.

She gave him five seconds and then she followed.

They moved through the main room and had just entered the kitchen when the overhead light came on.

Jamie blinked.

Poe leaned against the sink, an apple in his hand. "Took you guys long enough to get back."

Abi growled and lowered his weapon. "I could have shot you," he warned.

"Good thing you didn't," Poe shot back.

Jamie skirted around Abi and the island to stand toe-to-toe with Poe. "What the hell, man? Where have you been?"

He smiled. "Good to see you too."

Now she was just steamed. "You disappear—leaving your phone as if you've been attacked and dragged away. What was I supposed to think?"

He had better have a good explanation. Right now her temper was pushing toward the out-of-control mark. This was not in any way shape or form the slightest bit comical.

"Your doctor's body double was on the move."

Abi made a face that said he wasn't buying it. "What exactly does that mean?"

"I took a walk. Early. I took those very nice binoculars you had in the kitchen down by the cliff and had myself a look around. While I was watching I saw someone run out of the house. He seemed in a panic." Poe shrugged. "Like the devil was after him."

"That happened this morning?" Jamie shook her head. "Yesterday morning, I mean?"

"That's right. When I zoomed in, I thought it was Case— Dr. Case. Two men—security, I presume—rushed out and tackled him."

"How do you know it wasn't Dr. Case?" Jamie glanced at Abi. The man she spoke with at the hospital had to have been the real Dr. Case…right? He hadn't actually done any surgery. He only met with the patient and viewed a CT scan.

Uncertainty swelled inside her. What if it wasn't him?

"I can't be certain, of course," Poe admitted. "But amid all the yelling—not that I could hear any of it well enough to understand what was being said—another figure appeared at the front door. I zoomed in and he, I think, was the real Dr. Case. He started pointing and barking orders, which would seem to confirm my initial conclusion. The two security thugs dragged the other *Dr. Case* into the house."

"How does this explain why you disappeared?" Abi asked, his distrust showing.

"Apparently, while I was watching this go down, there was another member of the security team watching me. I took off in a direction away from the house so he would hopefully believe I had come from a different location. I dropped my phone and didn't want to risk going back for it."

"So where have you been?" Jamie demanded.

"Well, I thought I was in the clear, but I ran right into the guy. He took me down to the house and that's where they kept me until about two hours ago."

Jamie had known Poe for a while now. She trusted him completely, but there was something wrong with this story. No, what was wrong was with the way he was telling it. "You're saying you've been held hostage all day and night?"

"In the basement. I could hear the music when the party was going on."

"How did you get away?" A cold hard knot formed in Jamie's gut. So maybe he was telling the truth.

"About nine o'clock last night, a guy walked in and told me I was free to go. I walked back up here, but the two of you were gone."

"I'm finding this a little difficult to believe," Abi said. He looked to Jamie. "Are you buying this?"

"Are you okay?" Jamie searched her friend's face. "I mean, really okay?"

He nodded. "I don't think they intended to shoot me or anything. They just wanted me out of the way for a while."

Jamie turned to Abi. "Can we be certain the man at the hospital was the real Dr. Case?" Damn, this was not good. Luke's life depended on them delivering the surgeon—the real, miracle producing one.

A single moment of hesitation elapsed and in that fleeting second, Jamie knew Abi was about to lie to her.

"I can't be certain."

Now Jamie was furious. "You said you could tell the difference."

"Wait, wait, wait," Abi argued, stepping forward, bellying up to the island, "I would need to be close to him to confirm it's really him. He has a birthmark."

"Oh. My. God. Birthmarks are like tattoos—they can be recreated. Faked!"

"Not this birthmark. It wouldn't be so easily faked. It's a deep scar beneath his ribcage. He could certainly have had it repaired at some point in his life if he'd chosen, but creating the same look wouldn't be an easy task—particularly if you only wanted it to be temporary."

Jamie told herself to remain calm. Arguing with him would accomplish nothing. "As long as you're certain."

"I'm certain."

"What're we doing now?" Poe asked. "I got the impression they thought I was the trouble they'd maybe heard a rumor about. Then they let me go. I figured whatever was supposed to happen had happened, but then you two came back. So apparently, it didn't."

"We were at the party prepared to carry out the mission and there was an emergency at the hospital and Case had to go there," Jamie explained. "He just got back home. We followed him there, then came here."

"Whatever happened over there this morning," Poe said, "and tonight, it feels like something totally unrelated to what we're here to do."

"Did you hear anything while you were there?" Abi asked, his own concern visibly growing.

"I was in the basement, so not much. Except there was a lot of moving around. Big sounds like furniture."

Jamie considered what she had seen at the doctor's home. "Everything appeared to be in place. It didn't feel like there were items missing."

Abi turned his hands up. "Maybe it was just the cleaning and prep for the gala."

Poe shrugged. "I guess so. I'm just saying that's about all I heard while I was down there."

"Were you provided with food and water?" Jamie could see them sending someone down with water at least.

"A guy brought a tray at lunchtime and then later in the evening—before the party started."

"You didn't see anyone else the entire time?" Abi pressed.

"No one."

"I need to think about this." Abi glanced at Jamie, then left the room.

The sound of the glass doors opening and then closing told Jamie he'd gone onto the patio, probably to watch the house below.

Poe looked at Jamie then. "There's something off with this. He's not telling us everything."

Jamie nodded. "At this point I don't think I can even pretend he's being completely up front." She looked directly at Poe then. "I was really, really worried about you. I walked the cul-de-sac." She exhaled a big breath. "I was scared that you were in real trouble."

Poe took her by the arm and ushered her toward the stairs. He looked to see that Abi was still on the patio. "Come with me."

They hurried up the stairs and into the en suite of the room Poe had been using. He closed the door and turned on the shower.

"That story I gave downstairs was for Abi."

Her anger flared again. She had suspected he was not telling the truth. "Poe, what does that mean?"

"It means I am worried about what's happening here. I do not trust this guy. He is lying about too many things."

Jamie waffled between thinking he could be right and lashing out. "What things exactly?"

"I talked to your grandmother."

His words stunned her. "What?"

"I told her my concerns and she did some digging. This guy Case didn't start out being the good savior surgeon that everyone thinks. He purposely only performed certain surgeries. The patients he chose paid him huge bonuses under the table. That's why he has a body double. He fears for his life. But that seems to be shifting so I don't know exactly what's happening. This is just part of the talk about him."

This was not what Jamie wanted to hear. It didn't represent the way Case had presented himself at the hospital.

"His body double is actually his identical twin brother. All of this—" he glanced at the door, then lowered his voice "—all of this is wrong. Whatever Abi is doing it's not what he says he's doing. If some rich guy wanted the surgery, all he would have to do is pay the bonus price."

Jamie thought of the Mason family. How could they

have paid a bonus for surgery? Why wouldn't someone—anyone—file a complaint about this?

"Your grandmother gave me this information," he said. "I couldn't have known otherwise. Her investigator, Ian Michaels, is here in case we need backup." He pulled a weapon from his waistband at the small of his back. "That's how I got this."

Jamie felt sick. "I'm not saying you or my grandmother is wrong, but there has to be an explanation. Abi wouldn't do this." There was bad and then there was *bad*. "And what you're saying about Case just doesn't fit with the man I met last night."

"I'm with you, Jamie. Whatever you decide. I swear I am. I just need you to think long and hard and decide if there's a chance you might be wrong."

"I get it." She did. She really did. "You have my word that I'm taking all that he says with a grain of salt."

"Good."

A knock on the door made them both jump.

"Is this a private party or am I invited?"

Jamie and Poe shared a look. Poe shut off the shower and opened the door. Abi walked in, making the bathroom seem far smaller than it had been moments ago.

"Who wants to tell me what's going on?" He folded his arms over his chest and leaned against the door frame.

"We've learned some information that seems to counter the intelligence you have," Jamie admitted.

Abi looked to Poe before meeting her gaze. "And where did you get this intelligence?"

"My grandmother." She squared her shoulders and crossed her arms over her chest. "I trust my grandmother implicitly."

"What is this intelligence?" He looked between the two of them again.

"Dr. Case is charging bonuses from the patients he chooses to help. His so-called body double is actually his identical twin brother."

Abi nodded. "Well, your grandmother's intelligence is not without merit."

Fury blasted Jamie. "You didn't think I needed to know any of this?"

"Well, there are mitigating circumstances that prevented me from telling you these things."

Jamie held up her hand. "Start from the beginning and tell me those things now. Right now."

"Shall we retire to the living room where it isn't quite so stuffy and humid?"

Jamie sidled past him. She had not been this furious in recent history. These two men were people she trusted. Well, Poe more so than Abi, but she trusted them both on some level. And one or both were yanking her chain in a very dangerous game.

If not for needing to stay in complete control for her brother's sake, she could definitely use a drink right now. This was beyond nuts. When she reached the great room, she couldn't sit down. Instead, she leaned against the bar and waited. Poe took a position next to her. Abi sat on the sofa with an I-see-how-it-is face.

"Dr. Case has an identical twin brother who was used as his body double when the need arose. And, for a while, it did appear that he was choosing patients who paid a bonus for his services. But then, about two months ago he learned that his twin brother was scamming his patients. He was pretending to be the surgeon and, in a way, filtering the patients. Only those who were prepared to pay a huge extra fee under the table were put on the surgeon's schedule. When he found out, Dr. Case chose not to press charges since the man was his brother. Instead, he warned that if his brother ever showed his face around him again, he would see that he paid for what he had done."

Jamie could see where this was going. "So the scam was discovered and remediated before your employer was in need of surgery. Since Dr. Case never chose patients in this way, he would cut off his hands before agreeing to such a thing."

"Exactly. Which leaves us with the plan as I've lain out to you already."

Jamie turned to Poe. "Sound plausible to you?"

Abi rolled his eyes. "Really?"

"I can see that scenario happening," Poe said, ignoring Abi. "Nothing the Colby Agency found opposes the possibility of that scenario."

"Knowing all that, what do we do now?" Jamie asked. "My brother is still caught in all this."

"While we were at the party," Abi explained, "I left a couple of bugs in the house. Popped a couple of tracking devices on cars. We're just waiting to hear there's movement."

"Is the Case's vacation still on?" Jamie asked. How long were they going to be in a waiting stance? She needed to find her brother and get him out of this mess.

"The vacation is still on. At some point this morning, the family is supposed to prepare to leave. The time is being withheld for reasons that are obvious."

"If the family loads up to go on vacation," Poe said, "there will be all manner of security involved. Are we going to end up in a shootout?"

"We are not. We will step in before they get into the family limo to make their escape," Abi explained.

"Have you spoken with your employer since the emergency fiasco? Any update on who this fake nurse was?" That still bugged Jamie.

"We have reason to believe someone else has decided to make an attempt on the doctor."

Having one desperate individual ready to cross so many lines to make something happen was one thing but to have two—at least—competing to achieve the same goal was more than a little disturbing.

"How do we know there won't be additional attempts?" Jamie started to pace. She couldn't help herself. The situation was not contained at all. There were far too many variables.

"We have no control over what others do," Abi argued. "We can only move forward with our own plan until some sort of roadblock pops up in our path and then we go around it." He looked directly at Jamie. "That's why I told my employer we needed the best."

This conversation was feeling repetitive. "I appreciate the vote of confidence, but this is far too risky for comfort."

Poe added, "My gut says that we should move on our own count and not based on the movements of others."

"Waiting could be a mistake," Jamie agreed. She turned to Abi. "It gives the other team more opportunity to try a second strike."

"We are not moving prematurely," Abi argued. "There is nothing to be gained by jumping the gun, so to speak."

"Let's talk about this," Jamie pushed back. "We just spent six hours at the hospital because someone posing as a nurse called in a fake emergency. Now, we're tired—the security supporting Dr. Case are no doubt tired as well. And we're standing around here as if we have all the time in the world and no one else is even thinking about this sort of thing."

"All right." Abi pushed to his feet. "I will call my employer and see if he will agree to our moving forward now."

He walked outside and closed the glass doors behind him.

Poe turned to Jamie. "We need to be prepared. Luke is depending on us to ensure this goes down right and, frankly, I'm losing any and all confidence in what he's doing."

"I'm with you and ready to go," Jamie assured him.

"I should call Victoria and let her know what's happening."

Jamie shook her head. "I should call her."

"Sure. She'll be happy to hear from you."

Jamie took out the cell and put through a call to her grandmother. It was even earlier in Chicago, but she wouldn't mind.

"Jamie, are you all right?"

She sounded so worried, and Jamie's chest ached at the idea. "I'm fine, Grandmother. We're on standby for the moment. We had a false alarm and the mission had to be delayed but we should be moving out soon."

"Poe is there with you now?"

"Yes, he is. He's updated me on everything."

"Good. I'm not sure Abi's employer is on the up-and-up, Jamie."

"I know. I'm worried about that too. Hopefully we'll know something soon. I'm ready to move."

"Just be careful. You have a guardian angel."

Jamie smiled. "I will, Grandmother. Don't worry, I know."

They said their goodbyes, and Jamie ended the call just as Abi returned from his private call.

"We will be moving out shortly," Abi announced. "We have a very short time for any final preparations."

"Thank God." Jamie took a breath. "I just need one last assurance from you, Abi, that this man—your employer— is properly prepared for the intentions he has laid out. This is a very delicate situation. If I note even the slightest hint that some untoward situation is going down, I will not help make that happen."

"No one," Abi insisted, "wants to keep Dr. Case alive more than my employer. You can rest assured that every precaution will be taken to protect him and his family."

Jamie turned to Poe. "Are you still prepared to do this? I will understand if you want to walk away. If any part of this goes wrong…"

There was no need to explain. Everyone in the room understood exactly what she was saying.

"I'm in," Poe said. "We do this together." He turned to Abi. "The three of us."

Abi nodded. "Thank you."

"Let's do it," Jamie announced.

Abi gave her a nod as well. "It is the right thing to do."

As long as no one died…she could live with doing whatever she had to do to save Luke.

She hoped that guardian angel her grandmother had sent was ready as well.

Chapter Thirteen

Lionheart Court,
7:00 a.m.

Jamie scanned the area around the house as the sun peeked above the trees.

It was almost time.

She, Poe and Abi hovered in a group of trees at the edge of the wooded area. Beyond their position was the land-scaped yard that surrounded the home of Dr. Case.

Half an hour ago they had received word that they should move into place. The three of them had come down the hill-side, which surprised Jamie. She'd expected to go in a ve-hicle, but Abi assured there would be a vehicle waiting for them when the time came. He had better be right.

"You're going in through the front," Abi said to Jamie. "Poe and I will approach from the rear."

Sounded easy enough. *Not.* "Do I have a cover?" Going in via the front door surprised her. Security was inside and around the house. Not just one or two either. They had al-ready established that there were a lot of security person-nel. Whoever answered the door was not going to let her in without one hell of a good explanation.

Abi smiled. "You talked to him at the hospital, did you not?"

The memory of the woman who'd started to cry in the waiting room pinged her, followed immediately by the flash of recall with Jamie and the doctor chatting in the room belonging to the woman's husband. Jamie had walked right into that one.

"I guess I did," she admitted.

Abi glanced at his watch.

When had he started wearing a watch? Apparently, he'd added it for the final step. She didn't recall him wearing one to the party. Change always set her on edge.

"You should go now." Abi turned to Jamie. "A car is coming up the driveway now. You're trading places with the driver."

Jamie spotted the headlights at the farthest end of the drive just before the two round orbs went out. "See you inside," she said to Poe before disappearing into the trees.

Sprinting through the trees wasn't so easy, but she managed. There was just enough daylight to prevent any head-on collisions with the flora or face-plants after tripping over roots. The car stopped as the driver somehow realized she was near. Probably a tracking device in the clothes she was wearing. Abi wasn't one to take chances. A good thing, she supposed.

The driver's-side door opened and the man behind the wheel emerged. He walked right past Jamie and into the woods without a glance or a word. Weird.

She watched until he'd disappeared and then she climbed into the car. Maybe she was accustomed to working with team members she knew and liked. This was strange territory.

After putting the car into Drive once more, she rolled slowly toward the house. When she reached the fountain that sat in the middle of the parking area, she slowed to a stop. By the time she put the car into Park and shut off the engine, a member of the security team was at her door.

She opened the door and started to get out, but he held up a hand. The weapon still sheathed on his hip warned that he was dead serious about her staying in the vehicle. "Let's see some ID."

"My name is... Jamie *Mason*. I'm here to speak with Dr. Case about his patient, my uncle, and what happened at the hospital last night."

He passed along a summary of what she'd said to who-ever was on the other end of his hidden communication device. A few seconds later he evidently received a re-sponse because he stepped aside and said, "You're cleared to come inside."

Jamie wondered again how Abi had set her up for this. How could he have known that she would approach the woman in the waiting room? Calculated guess? The idea also made her wonder if the whole thing had been a setup. Clearly, the incident with the patient had been... But the wife in the waiting room? Had the fake nurse sent her to the waiting room rather than allow her to stay in the room? Made sense if the supposedly accidental meeting between her and Jamie was the plan.

She followed the guard to the front door. He led her into the entry hall and then disappeared back through the door they'd entered.

Eight, no ten suitcases of varying sizes were lined up in the entry hall ready to be loaded into a vehicle. The family was ready to head off to some ski slope loaded with fresh white snow or some city glittering with ritzy shops. Maybe she should take a vacation. Her parents were in Europe. She couldn't remember the last time she'd actually taken a vacation. Or a holiday for that matter.

She traveled extensively with her work but that wasn't the same.

At all.

Work usually involved being stuck in some location where the target could be monitored 24/7. Once she'd spent days in a jail cell with a target for a cellmate. It was almost Christmas, and she had no idea if she would even be spending it with family, maybe her grandparents, or completely alone.

If you can't save your brother...what difference does the holiday make?

She blinked away the thought and focused on what she had to do. Dr. Case was the key to rescuing Luke. She had to keep that in mind above all else.

Movement at the far end of the larger hall snagged her attention. She focused on the man striding her way. *Dr. Case.* At least she hoped it was the real Dr. Case. What if it was his twin brother?

She steeled herself against the worries and readied to spin a tale that would keep her in the house until Abi and Poe showed up. At least she assumed that was the point.

"Ms. Mason." Case studied her a moment, a frown working its way across his forehead. "I checked on your uncle a little while ago and he was doing fine."

"He is," Jamie agreed. "One of the nurses said you and your family were leaving for an extended vacation and I really felt it was important that I speak with you before you go."

"I wouldn't call this an extended vacation," he offered. "We'll be gone the rest of this week and through the weekend, but I'll be back at the hospital on Monday." He studied her another moment. "What is it you need to speak with me about?"

Damn it, Abi. Come on.

"The nurse," she said. "The one who triggered the false alarm. Johnson, I believe her name was."

He nodded. "The hospital is working with the police in conducting an investigation. To my knowledge she hasn't been found as of yet."

"I think I saw her back at the hospital this morning and I didn't know who to tell." This obviously was a lie, but she was winging it. If she had to buy much more time, she wasn't sure how that was going to go down. The doctor was clearly already suspicious, and she was basically holding her breath.

He reached into his pocket and withdrew his cell phone. "Did you inform security?" He tapped the screen and pressed the phone to his ear.

"I told the nurse on duty at the desk—the one near my uncle's room."

For a few seconds, Case was preoccupied discussing her assertion with whomever he had called. Then he thanked the person and ended the call.

"Security is keeping an eye on everyone who enters the building. There has been no sign of her coming through any of the entrances."

Jamie made a face. Damn. Of course they were monitoring the comings and goings after the incident. "Well then, maybe she never left."

This appeared to give him pause. He withdrew his phone and made a second call. He passed along this suggestion, then hung up.

"Thank you," she said before he could start asking her questions. "I was just really worried about my uncle's safety, and I wasn't sure anyone would actually listen to me. You seemed so kind and so concerned. I felt the need to come straight to you. I'm so sorry for the intrusion."

"Daddy! Daddy!"

Lillian rushed into the room. Her pink sweatshirt sported a popular cartoon character. The pockets of her jeans were trimmed in pink and then there were the furry pink boots. The kid liked pink for sure. She glanced at Jamie, then smiled.

If the kid recognized her…

"This must be your daughter," Jamie said before the child could say a word.

Case smiled. "This is Lillian. She's very excited about the trip."

Jamie smiled. "Well, anyway, thank you, Dr. Case, for hearing me out and making sure my concerns are taken seriously."

This was it. She was out of time and options.

"Have a nice holiday, Ms. Mason."

"I thought your name was Jasmine."

Jamie's pulse reacted to the girl's statement, but she kept her smile in place. "That's right. Jasmine Mason. Most people call me Jamie."

The child frowned as if she wasn't sure that was correct.

"Have a lovely vacation," Jamie offered before turning to the door.

"How do you know Ms. Mason?"

Jamie cringed at the question he'd asked his daughter. The doctor realized something was off.

"We talked about the books," Jamie said, turning back to them and using a last-ditch effort to control the narrative.

Come on, Abi. Damn it.

"I told her about the ducks," Lillian said, her cheeks turning pink again. "I think she liked the idea."

"I absolutely did," Jamie said.

The front door suddenly burst open, and Jamie almost sighed with relief.

But the man who barreled over the threshold wielding a weapon was not Abi or Poe. Not unless they had found ski masks to don after parting ways with her.

"On the floor," he shouted.

Lillian threw herself against her father.

"What's going on?" Case demanded. "Rodgers!"

"Rodgers is not coming," the man in the mask said. "And neither is anyone else on your security team. Now get on the floor. Face down!"

He pointed the weapon at Lillian. "Now!"

Case lowered to his knees, taking his daughter with him. "Let's do as he says, Lilly."

Jamie was sinking to her knees when the guy pointed a look in her direction. "You," he ordered, "take the kid and wait outside."

"What?" Jamie pretended not to understand. Where the hell were Poe and Abi?

"Do it!" The masked man nudged the kid with his foot.

Lillian cried out. Her father tried to pull her into the protection of his body.

"It's okay, Lillian," Jamie said as she moved in the girl's direction. Jamie kept her attention fixed on the guy with the gun. "We'll just step outside for a minute."

More bodies flooded the entry hall. Two, no, three more wearing the same masks. All armed. What the hell was going on?

"Take the kid outside," the first man repeated.

"Come on, Lillian." Jamie offered her hand.

Dr. Case stared up at her, his grip firm around his daughter's arm. "What're you doing?"

Jamie looked directly into his eyes and tried her best to

show him with her own that he could trust her. "Whatever it takes to stay alive." Lillian took Jamie's hand. "I'm not going to let anything happen to you," Jamie promised. She shifted her attention to the man with the gun. "We're going outside like you said."

He jerked his head toward the door. "Now!"

Jamie held on tight to the girl's hand. She hovered close to Jamie, her slim body shaking with fear. Outside, two more cars had arrived. They sat askew as if they'd skidded to stops and were left where they landed.

Since the guy in the mask hadn't given any specific instructions about what they were to do once they were outside, Jamie hurried around the far left corner of the house and disappeared into the landscape, using mature shrubs and miniature trees as cover.

The girl was sobbing now. "Where are we going?"

Jamie drew her down into a squat behind a clump of large shrubs. "Be as quiet as you can," she whispered. "We don't want them finding us out here."

"What about Mommy and Daddy?"

Jamie hadn't seen Mrs. Case. "Was your mommy upstairs?"

Lillian nodded. "She told Daddy she had one more bag to pack."

"Okay. Let's stay calm and see what we can find out." Which really meant stay put until Jamie could figure out what the hell was going on.

So far she'd heard no gunshots—always a good thing. But where the hell were Abi and Poe and whatever backup Abi had put in place or ordered or whatever? Everything had fallen apart and she had no clear idea of what to do from here…except protect the child.

Jamie gauged the distance to the car she'd arrived in. It

was still parked near the fountain. If she could reach that car, she could take the child out of here, tuck her away in the Excalibur house and then come back to see what she could do with the unexpected takeover in the doctor's house.

None of what was happening made sense.

She leaned closer to Lillian and explained, "I need to get you someplace safe."

"We can't leave Mommy and Daddy," she whimpered.

"Listen to me, Lillian," Jamie whispered with all the urgency she could muster. "I can't help your mom and dad while I'm taking care of you. I need to settle you someplace safe so I can help them. That's what they would want. Trust me."

"I can't leave them," the girl insisted.

Shouts echoed from the front of the house. The door was open again. Someone was coming out or going in. Judging by the furiously raised voice, the coming or going—whichever it was—was not voluntary. Jamie listened intently to make out the words. Someone was not happy with how something had been done.

"Find her!"

She heard those words clearly.

"Now!"

They were looking for Lillian. A new wave of tension poured through Jamie. She considered the distance from their hiding places to the woods. It wasn't the direction she'd wanted to go, but she was out of options and quickly running out of time.

Jamie pressed a finger to the little girl's lips. Hoped she understood that it was imperative that she didn't make a sound.

If they could make the tree line, Jamie would find the

way to the house. She would call Victoria, then Ian Michaels. Poe had said he was close by. He could help.

Jamie clasped Lillian's hand in hers and gave it a squeeze. She leaned closer once more and whispered, "We're going to try and make it up the hill through the woods. Just be careful where you step and stay close to me and try not to make a sound."

Lillian nodded her understanding.

Holding tight to her hand, Jamie headed for the tree line. She wanted to go faster, but she wasn't sure how Lillian would do, so she set her pace to match the girl's.

The beam of a flashlight suddenly obstructed their view.

"Hold on there," a voice commanded.

Not Poe. Not Abi.

Damn it.

Jamie froze. Lillian did the same, gluing herself to Jamie's side.

"You were supposed to wait by the cars."

"No one told me where to wait."

"Well, I'm telling you now. Let's go?"

The beam of the flashlight shifted and in the moments it took her vision to adjust, she spotted the weapon in his hand.

"Fine," Jamie said, feigning frustration. She wasn't really sure what her part was supposed to be in this. Did they think she was someone else? Maybe the nanny who was on vacation. Who knew if their intel was up to par. Either way, it was best to play along until she had a better grip on what was going down.

The man with the gun ushered them back to where the two poorly parked cars waited. Another of the team opened the back passenger door.

"Get in," their guide ordered.

Jamie ushered Lillian into the car and slid in next to her.

"What about Mommy and Daddy?" Lillian cried softly.

"I'm sure they'll be fine," Jamie lied. What else could she do? No doubt these thugs were here for Dr. Case. He was far more valuable than anything else they might find in that house.

Jamie just couldn't say what the intent was.

For now, the only choice was to ride this out and see where they landed.

8:15 a.m.

THE DRIVER HAD stopped at the end of the long driveway leading away from the Case home and forced Jamie to put a sack over her head as well as one over Lillian's. Then they'd driven away. Upon arrival at their destination, an older house and certainly nothing in any of the subdivisions near the Case home, they'd been allowed to remove the sacks. A quick glimpse at the digital screen on the car's dash showed they had driven nearly twenty minutes and approximately twelve miles. The new location had to be something off a different road. Jamie had tried to keep up with the turns. There had been about four. A couple of lefts and a right, possibly a second right or at the very least a slight fork to the right.

The driver had then sequestered Jamie and Lillian to a bedroom inside the new location. Evidently the house was unoccupied since there was no bed, just an old futon. The place appeared to have been empty for a while considering the dust and cobwebs. Not to mention it smelled musty.

"I'm scared." Lillian hugged herself. "I need to go home."

Jamie pulled her into her arms and held her close. "I will get you home, Lillian. Don't worry about that."

Jamie had seen only one guy. But he had a weapon. Still, he couldn't be everywhere all the time. All Jamie needed was an opportunity to make a move. She was banking on the idea that Abi would have planted a tracking device on her somewhere. He was too careful—too determined to cover all the bases—not to do so. At least she could hope.

One way or another, Jamie intended to get this child out of danger.

The sound of the guy's voice drew her to the wall between the bedroom and whatever lay beyond it. She cupped a hand, pressed it to her ear and then to the wall.

"We're here. Yes."

He was checking in. If Jamie was lucky, he would give away something about the plan. There had to be a plan.

Another issue she tried not to dwell on was what this situation would do to their timeline. Luke's face flashed in her mind. How long would it be before whoever had taken Luke would lose patience? Or maybe decide to cut his losses? Her gut clenched at the idea.

Not going there. Not yet.

"We'll be ready," their captor said. "Yes. Half an hour. Good."

Something was happening in half an hour.

Were they moving to a different location?

Jamie couldn't wait around to see what that would entail. Not to mention there was a strong possibility help would be coming to assist with the move. She needed to get the kid out of harm's way before any sort of backup arrived. She could not just wait around, assuming Abi would have her location and he or Poe would come to their rescue.

Her odds were far better right now, in this one-on-one situation.

She glanced at the girl. Keeping Lillian safe complicated everything. But if Luke were here, he would tell her to protect the kid at all costs.

Jamie drew in a deep breath and walked to the door and banged on it. "I need the bathroom."

A cliché request, but if it worked, she could live with it.

After the sound of something metal being handled—a lock maybe—the door opened. The man still wore his mask. That was a good thing. It meant he didn't want them to be able to identify him. To some degree, this suggested there was a perception that the hostages would at some point be released. Otherwise, what would revealing his face matter?

"Down the hall." He jerked his head left.

Jamie reached for the girl's hand.

"No. She stays here."

Jamie shook her head. "She's scared. She needs to stay with me. We're only going into the bathroom."

"If you give me any trouble," he warned, "I will kill you both."

"Don't worry. We're not going to give you any trouble."

Lillian clung to Jamie as they made their way to the end of the hall. Jamie took in all the details she could of their location as they made the short journey. Typical ranch house with a narrow hall. The doors along the hall opened into the three bedrooms—all basically empty like the one they'd been locked in. The final door, at the end of the hall, was a bathroom that sported generic beige tile along with harvest gold fixtures.

"Don't close the door all the way," he ordered.

"Got it."

In the bathroom, she left the door ajar. "Why don't you go first?" Jamie suggested.

While Lillian did her business, Jamie studied the small

room. There was a window, but it looked painted shut. Getting out the window wouldn't likely be easy. She checked behind the shower curtain and under the sink, careful not to alert their keeper.

When Lillian was done, Jamie relieved herself, using that time to continue her study of the small room.

Once they had washed their hands and exited the room, she asked, "Any bottled water around here?"

"You couldn't get a drink from the sink?" He gestured to the bathroom.

Jamie shrugged. "No cup or glass."

He swore and stamped back down the hall. Jamie took Lillian's hand and followed him. The hall opened into a small living room that fronted a kitchen-dining combination. The rest of the house was unfurnished other than a couple of plastic chairs. Definitely vacant. Probably a rental.

In the kitchen there was a six-pack of bottled water on the counter. No dust, which told her it had been provided for this operation.

"You can each have one but don't ask for anything else."

Jamie passed a bottle of water to Lillian and then took one for herself. "Thank you."

"When are my mom and mad coming?" Lillian asked.

The man looked at her for a long moment. He grabbed a bottle of water for himself, twisted off the top and took a long swig. Then he said, "Don't worry, kid. As soon as we get what we need, you'll be back with your family and on the way to your fancy vacation."

Wouldn't it be great if it were that simple? The trouble was that Jamie couldn't assume he was telling the truth.

"Let's go," he said with a gesture toward the end of the house where the bedrooms were.

Holding Lillian's hand, Jamie led her back to the bedroom. She'd been right. A padlock had been added to the door. Once they were inside, he locked it.

Jamie slowly walked the perimeter of the room. This bedroom was on the back side of the house. She peeled back the dusty paper that had been taped to the window. She squinted to see beyond the dirty glass. The overgrown grass in the small backyard led right up to the woods. Definitely an advantage.

Next, she checked the lock on the window. It moved. She set it to the unlock position. The window was an old one—wood, not vinyl or aluminum. The screening was long gone. The issue with wood windows was if they had been painted without being moved up and down afterward, then often, they were glued shut. Not so terrible if one had a utility knife with which to cut them loose.

She turned to Lillian and leaned close to whisper in her ear. "Talk to me about the vacation. Try to sound natural."

Lillian nodded and started talking. "We're going to New York."

"Wow, that sounds exciting." Jamie braced herself, her hands on the wood sash. She pushed. The sash didn't budge.

She took a breath and tried again. Pushing upward with all her strength. The sash moved the tiniest bit, giving her hope.

"I hope it snows," Lillian was saying. "We almost never get snow here."

"That would be nice," Jamie said. She readied herself and tried again. This time the sash moved about three inches.

While Lillian went on about all the sites in New York she wanted to see, Jamie braced her hands on the bottom of the sash this time and shoved upward.

The window went up another four or five inches.

Jamie glanced toward the door and nodded to Lillian to keep going. Then she shoved one last time with all her might.

The sash went up as far as it would go. Jamie shook her arms to release the throbbing tension.

Now all they had to do was climb out.

Jamie went first. She surveyed the backyard but saw nothing of concern. She motioned for Lillian to climb out.

"I'm sure your mom will take you shopping." Jamie talked while she helped her make the drop onto the other side.

"I hope so," Lillian said, her eyes wide with worry.

Jamie glanced left. Not that way because they would have to pass the kitchen window and the back door.

She pointed right and to the woods. Then she leaned close. "Keep as quiet as possible, but move as fast as you can."

Lillian nodded.

Jamie took her hand and started moving away from the house that was to have been their prison…or maybe their grave.

Chapter Fourteen

Stonewall Drive, Nashville,
9:50 a.m.

Kenny struggled to control his anger until they had the doctor and his wife settled in the great room of Amar's employer. Another rich guy, apparently, who had decided his life was more important than the doctor's, the Case family's or any-damned-one else's.

But that wasn't really the reason Kenny felt so furious. He was mad as hell because Amar had seen trouble coming and he had hesitated long enough that Jamie and the doctor's kid had been taken by the other team—the other set of bad guys.

Kenny walked out onto the terrace where he could properly pace and mutter the swear words burning inside his throat.

Like the doctor's home, there was a pool and all the usual trappings of überwealth. The home was older than the one on Lionheart Court, but the location was likely the draw. Kenny shook his head. What the hell was he doing here?

They had kidnapped a surgeon and brought him to this place.

He told himself he'd made the right decision. Jamie's brother was being held hostage. It wasn't like he could ignore the situation and he sure as hell didn't trust Abidan Amar to straighten this out. So he'd come along. He'd dove in and done what he could to help. For Luke. For Jamie.

Now Jamie was missing too.

The French doors opened, and Amar joined him on the terrace. Kenny looked away, not trusting himself to look the guy in the eye.

"We have a problem," Amar announced.

Kenny wheeled on him. "You think? Like who the hell took Jamie and the kid? Do you have a handle on that situation?"

"Unfortunately, I can't say who took them. A competitor it seems who isn't looking to save a life, but is positioning himself for a ransom demand."

Kenny took a breath and told himself not to punch the guy. Doing so would not fix the situation and right now they needed to figure out how to help Jamie and that little girl. This was not the time to allow emotions to reign.

Of course Amar couldn't say who had taken Jamie and the kid. He'd totally missed whatever happened this morning. He and his people should have picked up on the trouble in the air.

"Your people were already on the ground when the other guys showed up—and there was only three of them. Three! They came in right under the noses of your people and walked away with Jamie and the girl."

If there was ever a situation that screamed of incompetence, this was it. Kenny struggled to regain his composure. Amar was not incompetent. Kenny knew this. He was just angry. Even the best plan could go awry. He also knew this firsthand. Rather than focus on pointing to how badly Amar had failed, they both needed to focus on how to rescue Jamie and the child.

"You are correct," Amar agreed. "There is no excuse for what happened except to admit that someone on my team failed. However, I've just been told that we have some security footage that may help us nail down who these people were and hopefully find them."

Kenny was over simply talking about this. They needed to act. To do that, he had to focus and to focus he had to find calm. "What is the problem you mentioned?"

"Dr. Case will not move forward with the surgery here until his daughter is found."

Well, Kenny didn't blame him. He'd been kidnapped. His family had been dragged from their home and his daughter had ended up God only knew where. Why would he cooperate? Only a fool would do so.

"What's your plan?" Surely the man had a strategy for straightening out this screwed up mess.

"I'm glad you asked." Amar's sly smile was more of a smirk, and it seriously rubbed against Kenny's last nerve. "We have someone waiting to see us downstairs in the game room."

Kenny followed him back into the house, beyond the great room and down the stairs to the walkout basement. It was like another house, the floor space no doubt as spacious as the layout upstairs.

Amar turned down a hallway to the left, which led into another large room with doors leading to the outside. A man wearing black, as they all had been this morning, was secured to a chair in the center of the room. He glanced at Kenny, then Amar, before looking away. His own smirk suggested he was not worried about whatever they had come to do.

Never a good sign.

"Mr. Reicher."

He turned to Amar as he approached, but said nothing.

Kenny stayed back a few steps and watched. This was Amar's show. He'd give him some time to see if he could pull this debacle together. Jamie liked the guy. Respected him. He must be better at this than he'd shown so far.

"Your girlfriend—Darla, I believe, is her name—and her baby are on the way here. Is there anything you'd like to share with us before they arrive?"

Reicher's face paled a little. "I have nothing to say."

Amar smiled. "Really. Darla says her baby is your son, Paul junior. She's very excited to bring him to see the Christmas surprise I told her you had arranged."

His face tightened. "She doesn't know anything about all this."

"That's too bad, Mr. Reicher. I think she may be very disappointed about what she finds here today."

He looked away a moment.

Kenny was out of patience. "That little girl your friends took better be safe," he warned, stepping closer. "If something happens to her…"

Reicher glared at Kenny. "She's fine. Nothing will happen to her if Dr. Case is delivered as requested."

Amar shrugged. "You see, Mr. Reicher, that is not going to happen. We have the doctor, and he is the important one. I'm sure you realize this. And as much as we want his daughter to be safe, she really is not our top concern."

Kenny bit his tongue to prevent calling him a liar. But he understood the tactic. He didn't like it, but he understood it.

"I don't think the doctor will see it that way," Reicher argued, the fear in his eyes impossible to conceal.

"I have a onetime offer for you, Mr. Reicher," Amar said. "You tell me where my friend Jamie and the girl are and—assuming they are unharmed—I will allow you to

leave with your girlfriend and your son when they arrive."
He laughed. "Hell, I'll even throw in a little bonus for that
Christmas surprise. But, if you waste this opportunity, there
is nothing I can do for you."

Kenny shook his head. "He doesn't deserve a deal. I say
we just beat it out of him."

"But I've already called Darla and she's on her way."
Amar checked his watch. "We have maybe ten minutes
before she arrives."

"Okay," Reicher said. "Just don't hurt her or tell her
about any of this."

That was easier than Kenny expected. Maybe too easy.
"Tell us where the girl and my friend are being held."

"They're in a house on Trinity Road. I can give you directions."

"How about you take my friend there," Amar suggested.
"That way there are no miscommunications."

"But what about Darla and the baby?"

"I'll let them know to go home and wait. You'll be there
soon."

Reicher looked from Amar to Kenny. "How do I know
I can trust either of you?"

Amar withdrew a knife, opened the blade and sliced it
through the bonds holding Reicher to the chair. "I suppose
you're just going to have to take a chance. If you're not willing to take a chance, then you're in the wrong line of work."

Kenny grabbed the guy by the collar. "Let's go." He
shoved him toward the door.

Amar leaned in closer to Kenny. "Once you have Jamie
and the girl, just leave him at the house and get back here.
We're running out of time."

Kenny nodded. "I just hope Jamie doesn't regret trusting you because I sure as hell do."

In the corridor before they reached the stairs, one of the men working on Amar's team approached Kenny and Reicher. "This way, gentlemen."

They were led to a door that opened into a six-car garage. Outside the garage, one of the black sedans Amar's people had used waited as if everyone had known this was the way things would work out.

"I'll be your driver," the man said as he opened the rear passenger-side door.

Kenny waited for Reicher to get in, then he dropped into the seat next to him. He removed his weapon and held it ready. "Don't waste my time," he warned Reicher.

Reicher gave the driver the street address.

The drive took longer than Kenny had hoped, but he didn't know a lot about the area. Trinity Road was closer to where they had been in the Excalibur house than where they'd ended up today. Staying in the same general vicinity as the home invasion for hostage containment made a sort of sense, he supposed.

Trinity Road led away from the more heavily populated areas and had older houses set back off the road. It was heavily wooded in some areas.

"Up ahead on the left," Reicher said.

When they turned onto the long drive, a man with a weapon emerged from the woods.

Kenny poked the muzzle of his weapon into Reicher's side. "Unless you want to die now, I would suggest you think carefully before you speak to this guy."

Reicher nodded, then, hand shaking, powered his window down. "I'm here to pick up the girl."

"Good luck with that," his comrade said. "That lady with her opened a window and they took off. I've been looking for them for the past hour."

Kenny's pulse thumped with the news. He barely resisted the urge to grin.

"We'll help you look for them," Reicher said. "Get in the car." He slid toward Kenny.

The other guy got in. As he closed the door, he looked at Kenny. "Who the hell are you?"

Kenny pressed the muzzle of his weapon to the man's forehead. "Toss your gun into the front seat."

He hesitated.

"Do it," Reicher said. "We're not going to win this one."

The new guy reluctantly did as ordered.

"Anyone else here?" Kenny asked.

The new guy shook his head. "Just me."

"Drive up to the house," Kenny said to the driver.

The car rolled forward, stopping at the small ranch house. Kenny and the driver emerged and ushered the two men into the house. Kenny walked through. Spotted the raised window in the bedroom and smiled.

"Go Jamie." He crossed to the window and surveyed the area into which the two had taken off.

Back in the living room, the driver had the two standing with their backs against the wall. Kenny looked to the driver. "You have anything we can use to secure these two so we don't have to shoot them?"

The driver nodded and hurried out of the house.

Kenny looked to the guy who had been guarding Jamie. "How long ago did they escape?"

"Maybe an hour."

Damn. They could be anywhere by now. Maybe even back at the Excalibur house. "If I don't find them, I'll be back."

When the two were secured, Kenny and the driver headed outside.

"Let's make sure they have to walk out of here if they somehow manage to get loose."

"Good idea," the driver agreed.

"What's your name?" Kenny asked while he slashed the tires.

"Landon."

"Well, Landon," Kenny said as he got back to his feet, "maybe we need the car's fob to ensure it's no use to anyone."

Landon nodded and went back into the house. Half a minute later, he returned with the car's fob. He popped the hood and did something under there. Kenny wasn't much of a mechanic so he had no clue what. He could change a tire and check the oil. That was about the extent of his vehicle maintenance skills.

When Landon closed the hood, he said, "They won't be going anywhere in this vehicle." Then he dropped the fob on the ground and used the heel of his boot to disable it as well.

"Take the car," Kenny decided, "drive slowly along the road. I'll walk and have a look around in the woods."

"You got it," Landon said.

Kenny scanned the overgrown grass and quickly spotted the signs of recent movement. He followed that path into the woods.

"Jamie!" If they were still in these woods, maybe they would hear him calling.

Once he was deeper in the woods, the path wasn't as easy to follow. He trudged through the underbrush and called Jamie's name over and over.

The sound of a car horn blowing had him stalling in his tracks. He listened. Coming from Trinity Road. Maybe Landon had found them.

Kenny started to run through the woods. When he

emerged, he was in the yard of another property. He kept close to the tree line along the yard's border since he had no desire to get shot. Then he saw Landon's car on the road. Kenny broke into a hard run.

As he reached the road and the car, the rear passenger window powered down. "Looking for me?"

Jamie. His knees almost gave out on him. "You and Lillian okay?"

She nodded. "We're good. Get in."

Kenny opened the front door and dropped into the seat. To Landon, he said, "Let Amar know we're headed back with what we came for." He turned to Jamie then. "Where were you?" He glanced at Landon. "How did he find you?"

"We were hiding in the church a mile or so up the road. The guy who'd been holding us had come through looking for us, but he didn't think to look under the altar."

Kenny laughed. "But you thought to hide there."

Landon ended his call. "Smart move," he said to Jamie. "I spotted the church as we drove in. When we were told you had escaped on foot, I figured you went to the church. That's where I would have gone."

Kenny had to admit he would probably have done the same. He looked to Lillian then. "Your parents are going to be very happy to see you."

She nodded. "Jamie saved me."

Jamie smiled. "We did it together."

Kenny was just thankful they were safe. He was pretty sure he'd never been so relieved in his life.

"I don't think that guy was very good at his job," Lillian suggested.

"We're just lucky he wasn't," Jamie pointed out. She looked to Kenny. "And we're very lucky that my friend is really, really good at his job."

Chapter Fifteen

Stonewall Drive,
Noon

Lillian wanted food so they had to stop. Thankfully, she recognized where they were pretty quickly once they were on the main road and directed the driver to her favorite drive-through. Jamie wasn't really hungry, but she understood the necessity of eating. She hadn't gotten any sleep, so forgoing food was not a good idea. She needed her head clear and her body energized.

"So this is the place." Jamie assessed the mansion where the doctor and his wife had been taken.

"This is it," Poe said, surveying the estate as the car parked in front of the house.

It wasn't as new as the doctor's mansion, but it was every bit as ostentatious in its own right. The whole situation was over the line. One rich guy kidnapping another to get what he wanted. How screwed up was that? Maybe growing up a Colby made her understand at a fairly young age how completely upside down the world could be, but there were still times, like this one, when she just couldn't get past the reality of how bad it really was. More than just upside down.

What was wrong with these people?

The part that bothered her the most in all this was that she actually got it. These people were desperate. Desperate people, no matter how wealthy, did desperate things, creating desperate situations.

Jamie got out of the car and held the door for Lillian. The girl was still shoving fries in her mouth when she got out. Poor thing, she really had been starving. Kids were like that. She remembered when she and Luke were that age. They were always clamoring for food—especially fast food.

The double front doors opened, and Abi stood in the doorway. "Welcome back."

Jamie's first thought was to punch him, but what kind of example would that set for Lillian? It was better if she behaved herself until the two of them had a minute alone to talk in privacy.

"Let's get this show on the road," Jamie shot back. "I'd like to see my brother."

Abi stepped aside and gestured for her to enter. "The doctor and Mrs. Case are waiting in the great room."

Lillian stuck close to Jamie as they walked through the entry hall and on to the great room. Like the Case home, the whole place was decked out for Christmas with a massive tree and tons of garlands. Under the tree, dozens of wrapped presents waited.

Mrs. Case gasped and rushed to her daughter. She paid no attention to Jamie, which was good. Dr. Case did the same.

Poe gave her a nod from the other side of the room. Jamie responded in kind. This was the best part of what they did—reuniting families or couples after a situation had pulled them apart. They didn't always get this moment.

After a good deal of hugging and weeping, Dr. Case

stepped back from his family and walked toward Abi. "Let's get this done."

"Very well." Abi gestured to the door. "You know the way."

Jamie glanced at Poe. "I'm going with them."

Poe nodded. "I'll hang around here."

Jamie hesitated. There were many things she wanted to say to him—things she probably should have said before now—but all of that would have to wait. Jamie needed to know what was happening with the doctor. This was the part that her brother's life depended upon. Poe would look after the daughter and the wife.

She wasn't allowing Abi or the doctor out of her sight until Luke was free. Whatever else happened, she intended to see that her brother was brought home safely.

Abi led the way down to the walkout basement area. There they walked through a massive game room and into a short corridor with no windows. At the end of that corridor was a door like one found on a bank vault. Jamie wasn't sure whether to be startled or impressed. Abi entered the code as if he'd been here many times before. Jamie decided she could safely assume the owner of this place was Abi's employer.

The door opened and they walked into a small curtained off area. The sort of space found in a mobile hospital setup. There was a sink, a temporary shower and a smaller curtained off dressing area. This, she surmised, was the prep area for the space beyond. No doubt a state-of-the-art surgical setup. Now she was totally impressed.

Case glanced back at Jamie and Abi and then started to strip off his clothes. He didn't need a block of instructions on what came next. Jamie turned her back and gave him some privacy. When the water in the small shower started running, she faced Abi once more.

"This guy has a surgical suite in his basement?" Was this for real?

"When he made the decision to go this route, he went all out."

Jamie shook her head. "This is way over-the-top, Abi."

The water in the shower stopped, preventing the need for Abi to respond. Jamie kept her back to Case as he dressed in what she presumed would be his surgical scrubs and gown. A sense of dread that would not be tamped down climbed into her throat. What if the patient died? Case was unquestionably a skilled and highly sought after surgeon who hadn't lost a single patient so far—according to his bio. But that didn't mean it couldn't happen. No matter that she and Abi had done what they were expected to do, would Luke still be released if the patient didn't make it?

Focus on the now, Jamie. Don't borrow trouble.

Case opened the curtained door and entered the surgery suite. The glimpse Jamie got of the room beyond this prep area was stunning. She couldn't imagine the money spent to prepare for this…but then, what was the value of a loved one's life? Most likely it was whatever a person possessed.

Abi gestured to the rack of scrubs. "If you're planning on going inside, you need to scrub down and dress for the occasion."

"We don't have to shower the way the doc did?" Jamie would be the first to admit that she could use a shower, but she didn't want to miss a moment of what was happening.

"Not unless you're planning to help with the surgery. But since he already has a nurse, another surgeon and an anesthetist, our assistance is not required."

Jamie gave a slow nod. "I'd like to see what's going on in there, considering I have a great deal to lose."

"Understandable." Abi peeled off his sweater, grabbed the bottle of Hibiclens soap and started the necessary process. Jamie did the same. They scrubbed down and pulled on surgical gowns.

When they stepped beyond the larger curtain, Jamie was almost startled. The lights. The equipment. It was incredible. The real thing—maybe even more state of the art than the average surgery suite found in hospitals. Right in the center of it all was a surgical table complete with the patient and surrounded by all the necessary equipment and, apparently, personnel. A clear enclosure separated that center area from the rest of the room. It was like a room with invisible walls inside a bigger room.

She watched as they prepared the patient—not an adult... a child. Her chest constricted.

As Abi had said, there were three people besides the surgeon, all suited in surgical gowns. Two working closely with the doctor, the other standing at the patient's head. The anesthetist.

The setup really was incredible. She shouldn't be surprised. If this was going to be done right, they needed not only the proper equipment, but also the proper personnel as well. No expense appeared to have been spared.

Another man, middle aged, stood well beyond the activity on the other side of the smaller surgical room. Was this the child's father?

Jamie leaned closer to Abi so she could whisper. "Is that him?" The doctor and those working around the patient were talking among themselves. She didn't want to distract or disturb them.

"Yes." Abi followed her lead, speaking in a whisper. "The father—my employer."

"Did you know the patient was a child?" Jamie understood that the patient's age didn't make what they had done right…but it somehow made it more palatable.

"I did. That's the only reason I agreed to the job."

Jamie's attention shifted to the ongoing procedure. The conversation between the doctor and those helping was so soft that she couldn't make out their words through those clear walls. It was the sounds of the machines that made her feel oddly discombobulated. Or maybe it was the whole situation that created such a sense of being overwhelmed.

"Should we go now?" She suddenly felt out of place even watching.

"I'm staying. You don't need to."

She nodded. "Okay. Going upstairs then."

Jamie exited the sterile environment, peeled off the surgical gown and pulled on her sweater. She tossed the gown into the provided hamper and opened the door. As she walked out, the door closed behind her, locking her out. She flinched at the sound or maybe it was the idea of what was happening in there.

Forcing her mind away from this thing they had done, she considered that she should call her grandmother and let her know she was okay and that the procedure was happening. Hopefully, Luke would be released soon. She shook herself. Good grief, it was Christmas Eve. She needed to see if anyone had heard from her parents.

One thing was certain—this was the most bizarre holiday of her life.

The trudge up the stairs was harder than she'd thought. She supposed she was more exhausted than she had realized or maybe all the emotions were just catching up with her. She had necessarily restrained her feelings related to Luke being held hostage. Now they were working overtime to bubble up.

Upstairs, Lillian and her mother were on the sofa in the great room, watching television. Mrs. Case looked as exhausted as Jamie. There was no shortage of guards. All dressed in black and stationed at every door and at the larger windows. Not just to keep the doctor in either. To keep new intruders out, she supposed.

Worry tugged at Jamie's brow. Where was Poe? She walked to the front door and had a look outside. No Poe out there. Then she walked back through the great room and on to the kitchen before she found him.

He stood at the island, a host of vegetables piled around him. He glanced up as she neared. "I decided to make a salad. Fast food never fills me up."

She went for a smile, but didn't quite feel it happen. "Sounds smart. Can I help?"

"You interested in cucumbers?"

"Sure. A salad isn't a salad without cucumbers."

She washed the long English cucumber and selected a knife. "Thick or thin slices?"

"Prepper's choice."

She thought about bringing up the morning's event and then the identity of the patient downstairs, but decided she needed to think on it for a while. There was a lot wrong with how those hours went down, but she couldn't be certain it had been what she now suspected.

Poe grabbed a couple of carrots and started to chop. He was very skilled.

"You've had lessons," she suggested.

"A class in Paris." He shrugged. "Another in Rome. I love to cook."

How had she not known that?

When they had prepped all the veggies and tossed them into a larger bowl, they cleaned up. The mundane work helped with the questions and emotions nudging at her. A little more *mundane* would be most welcome.

Poe tossed the hand towel on the counter by the sink. "I'll see if anyone is hungry."

"Do you have a cell phone? The guy who drove us to the other location took mine."

"Sure. Amar gave me another." Poe passed his cell to her. "I'm glad you're back, Jamie."

"Me too."

"I was worried. Really worried."

She nodded. "I've worried a lot during this thing."

He held her gaze for a moment longer as if he had more to say, then turned and headed for the great room.

Jamie had a feeling they both had things they needed to say.

She walked to the sink and stared out the window as she entered Victoria's number. As always, her grandmother answered on the first ring. "It's me," Jamie said since the number would not be familiar.

"I'm so grateful to hear your voice. Are you all right, Jamie?"

"I'm fine. Tired, but fine. The surgery is taking place now. Hopefully, Luke will be released soon."

How was it that saying the words almost made this thing feel like it was a normal mission? This was not normal. It was not even close to normal. They had broken a good number of laws, not to mention they had kidnapped a man and his family from the other thugs who had attempted to kidnap them. Add to that how someone on the opposing team had kidnapped her and the girl and they'd had to escape.

How crazy was that? Worse, she still couldn't even begin to fathom what the coming ramifications would be.

Mrs. Case and Lillian came into the kitchen with Poe. He served them both as if he'd trained at a five-star restaurant. Even when Lillian insisted there should be meat on a salad, he managed to rummage in the refrigerator and find deli slices of turkey, chopped it and added it to Lillian's salad.

The man was good. He was kind. Jamie smiled. And handsome.

"I can send the jet for you and Luke when you're ready," Victoria insisted, drawing Jamie's attention back to the call. "I'm anxious to have you both home."

That was the thing. No matter where Jamie lived and worked, Chicago would always be home.

"Sure." Whatever Victoria wanted to do would be fine by Jamie. At this point any sort of vacation from her everyday life would be great. "Have you spoken to Mom and Dad today?"

"I did and I'm so happy to say they'll be coming home tomorrow. They've decided that as much as they've enjoyed their little getaway, that Christmas is about being at home with family. I didn't tell them what was happening with Luke. I'm hoping the two of you will be here by the time they arrive and that this whole nightmare will be behind us."

Jamie hoped so as well. "I'll call you as soon as I lay eyes on Luke."

They exchanged goodbyes and Jamie took Poe's phone back to him. "Thank you."

"Everything all right with your grandparents?" He heaped salad onto a plate.

"Yes, and she just told me that my parents are coming

home tomorrow so it'll be a good day." As long as she got Luke back home safely.

He passed her the plate. "Eat."

Jamie thanked him and joined the Case family at the island.

Mrs. Case set her fork aside and turned to Jamie.

Jamie braced for her fury. Not that she could blame the woman. Look what they had done to her family…to their holiday plans. The thought sickened her. She couldn't tell the family that she'd only taken part in this because her brother's life was at stake. They certainly didn't need any added stress after all they'd been through. Besides, what kind of excuse was that? Who was to say whose family was the more important one?

No one…because that was not true any way you looked at it.

"Lillian told me about how you helped her escape that man. How you helped her run to safety and to hide."

Jamie managed a smile that felt like an imitation at best. "It was a team effort." She and Poe shared a look. She suspected he didn't feel heroic any more than she did.

Lillian blushed. "You're a superhero. Like in the movies."

"You were pretty heroic yourself, Lillian. You were strong and brave. You should be very proud of what you did too. Like I said—a team effort."

Mrs. Case smiled a weary expression as she turned back to her salad. Jamie felt sick at the idea of what she must be thinking. Though the woman was obviously grateful that Jamie had helped her daughter, she likely recognized as well that Jamie was part of the original kidnapping crew. That reality couldn't be ignored.

Lillian picked at her salad, eating mostly the turkey, before skipping back into the great room to resume the movie she'd been streaming.

Poe took his salad and followed her.

Jamie forked the greens and took another bite. She generally liked salad, but it all tasted bland today. She suddenly wished she had gone with Lillian and Poe. Sitting here with Mrs. Case and feeling what was no doubt the weight of her mounting accusations was not exactly sparking her appetite.

After an entire minute of silence, the older woman said, "My husband is very upset. He feels this entire event is a travesty."

It was actually, and Jamie wasn't going to try to excuse her actions. She had done what she had to do to keep her brother safe. She wouldn't do things any differently if she had to do it over and over again.

"He has," Mrs. Case went on, "tried very hard not to think of all the patients he can't save. He is only one man. But it has been very difficult. The burden of all those other lives has weighed heavily on him. Particularly in light of what his brother did for months before we realized what he was up to."

She didn't explain further, and Jamie didn't ask. She was already aware of the twin brother's deceit.

Mrs. Case went on, "The past few hours have driven that point home. It's one thing to know what's happening, but another altogether to be faced with the reality."

Jamie could only imagine how horrifying the ordeal had been and the number of emotional levels that horror had hit. As Mrs. Case had already said, the weight of having to turn patients away was awful enough, but to be forced to look at a child who desperately needed that help, and whose father was willing to do anything to make it happen, was immeasurably painful.

Working hard to keep her voice steady, Jamie confessed, "I will tell you I am not proud of the part I played in this. But—"

"If you hadn't," Mrs. Case argued, "my daughter might be dead. My husband might even be as well. Or me. You and your people kept us safe."

Jamie opted not to correct her. Yes, she, Poe and Abi may have provided a buffer between the Case family and the bad guys from the other team, but the truth was they weren't that different. They'd all been here for the same goal ultimately—to get Dr. Case to do what they wanted.

"They wanted twenty million dollars," Mrs. Case said. "For our daughter."

"There was a ransom demand?" Jamie wasn't aware that had happened, but she wasn't entirely surprised.

"Oh yes. Once you and Lillian were taken away, another man informed us of what they expected. We had twelve hours to pull the money together—which was absolutely ludicrous—before they were going to kill Lillian."

"Wow…that's terrible." Jamie replayed those minutes over in her head. The men had operated on a reasonably professional level. They had appeared prepared for what they had come to do…mostly. "They told me nothing. I had no idea."

"Your people saved us—*you* saved our daughter."

As much as Jamie appreciated being called a hero, there were some things that didn't add up for her. First, a twenty-million-dollar ransom demand should have come with a bigger team. What kidnapper who believed an asset was worth twenty million dollars only sent along one guard with that asset?

This was wrong somehow. Frankly, everything that had gone down felt wrong on some level.

There had been just three in the other crew in the first place. Three. With a twenty-mil ransom demand. Oh yeah, there was something very wrong with this situation.

Poe came to the door. "Jamie." He hitched his head toward the great room.

Jamie produced a smile, one slightly more real this time, for Mrs. Case. "Excuse me." She slid off her stool and went to the door. "What's up?"

"We need to talk."

She followed him beyond the great room to the entry hall. The guard there seemed to sense their need for privacy and stepped outside to monitor the door from there.

Poe glanced around. "Something is off with what happened this morning."

"I couldn't agree more." She hitched a thumb toward the kitchen. "The wife just told me there was a ransom demand for Lillian. Twenty million dollars."

Poe shook his head. "That's crazy. One of those guys— from the two left behind when the one took you and Lillian—basically split after you two were gone. Abi called in a backup crew to clean up the mess, but let's face facts, we already had more than three—besides us—here in the first place, which begs the question, how were we overtaken by three thugs?"

Jamie had an idea about that. "I think it was a setup to make the Cases believe we're the good guys."

"You mean we're not," Poe said with a shake of his head. "Don't answer that. I already know what we've been in this op." He blew out a big breath.

This was just another aspect of this whole business that weighed on Jamie. "I shouldn't have let you get involved with this."

He harrumphed. "Like you could have stopped me."

"We just have to make sure the rest of this goes off without a hitch. The family gets taken back home and no one dies."

Her chest tightened as she thought of Luke.

Keep him safe.

3:00 p.m.

By the time the doctor and Abi surfaced, Lillian had fallen asleep, and her mother was pacing the floor.

Jamie wasn't sure what would happen next, but if they were all lucky, it wouldn't involve the police. Or worse, the FBI, considering they had kidnapped the doctor and his family.

"How did it go?" Mrs. Case asked, looking tattered around the edges.

Dr. Case gave her a nod. "Very well. I'll be seeing him when we return from our vacation for a follow up. Until then, the doctor who assisted me will keep an eye on him. But I'm not anticipating any issues."

Jamie shared a look with Poe. That was certainly not the announcement she'd anticipated.

"A car will be here for you and your family in ten minutes," Abi explained.

Wait. Wait. Was this it? No accusations. No cops. No nothing?

Dr. Case turned to Abi. He looked from him to Poe, then to Jamie. "I realize what has happened today. Don't doubt that I am fully aware." His gaze lit the longest on Jamie.

This was the part she had been expecting...dreading.

"But in reality, all the three of you took from my family were a few hours of our time." He glanced at his daughter. "I wonder if you—" he looked from Jamie to Poe and then Abi again "—had not made the decision to help the child downstairs, what would have happened to our family? Those other men were clearly unconcerned for the safety of my family. Their only desire was money." He shook his head, regret clear on his face. "The idea that my work has come to this tears me apart. Anyone who needs the help I can provide should be able to have it without such theatrics. This has opened my eyes to what I know I must do next. It wasn't bad enough what happened before…" He heaved a heavy breath. "The only answer is that more surgeons must be trained in this procedure. It's the only way to see that we meet the need of all…not just that of certain patients." He exhaled a weary breath. "Thank you for helping me to see this more clearly."

Abi nodded, but said nothing. He turned to Jamie and motioned for her and Poe to follow him to the kitchen. They gathered around the island.

"A car will be arriving shortly." He set his gaze on Jamie's. "The driver will take you to your brother's condo. Luke will be delivered there at approximately the same time." He turned to Poe then. "If you need a different car, just say the word."

"I'm going with Jamie." Poe looked to Jamie. "We have a mission report to complete."

Abi nodded. "Very well." He smiled. "We make a good team."

Jamie laughed. "Except for the fact that you were keeping all sorts of details from us." She leaned in closer and spoke more quietly. "Like the three guys from this morning. Give me a break. After the doctor's monologue in there, you really expect me to believe that was a coincidence? And where did you find them? Thugs-R-Us?"

Abi didn't smile, but the twinkle of amusement in his

eyes was unmistakable. "No one is calling the police," he said. "In my humble opinion, that implies it was a brilliant strategy."

"You couldn't have warned us?" Poe argued, sounding more than a little ticked off.

Abi bumped him on the shoulder with the side of his fist. "The goal was authenticity. It's hard to fake, wouldn't you say?"

Poe held up a hand. "Whatever."

"In any case," Abi said, "thank you for your help. Your car will be here any moment." He smiled at Jamie. "You'll be pleased to find Ian Michaels behind the wheel."

Whoa. Now wait a minute. "How did you get in touch with Ian?" Poe had told her that Victoria had sent Ian to provide any necessary backup, but that was the last she'd heard about him being here. Too much had gone down for her to even think about Ian. She decided it might be best not to mention this to her grandmother's long time loyal investigator.

"I called your grandmother," Abi explained. "I told her you would be ready to depart within the hour and she said Michaels would pick you and Poe up for transport back to Chicago." He chuckled. "She also invited me to your Christmas party. Unfortunately, I'm unavailable. I'm sure you understand."

"Of course. You're a busy man." Jamie barely resisted the urge to roll her eyes.

"One more thing," Abi said. "For the record, the ransom demand for Luke…" He shrugged. "Just a little something for more of that authenticity."

Jamie did roll her eyes that time. "Good to know." She extended her hand. "Until we meet again, Abi."

He gave her hand a shake. "I am certain we will." He turned to Poe next and extended his hand.

"I, for one," Poe said, "hope to never see you again."

Abi laughed. "I'm confident that can be arranged."

When the first car arrived, Jamie, Poe and even Abi stood on the portico and waved goodbye to the Case family. As the car drove away, Lillian turned around in her seat and waved some more. Jamie kept waving until the car was out of sight.

"This must be the enigmatic Mr. Michaels," Abi said as a second car rolled up to the house.

Jamie turned to face her old friend. "Take care of yourself, Abi."

He hugged her. She didn't resist. Given their occupations, it could easily be the last time they saw each other.

Poe only allowed the other man a nod before walking away.

Ian emerged from behind the wheel and gave Jamie a hug. "I am so glad to see you," she admitted.

"Always." Ian drew back. "Let's go pick up your brother."

Jamie and Poe relaxed in the back seat as Ian drove away, though it was impossible to relax completely until she laid eyes on her brother.

The drive to his condo felt like a lifetime and when they arrived, Luke was sitting on the front steps. Jamie rushed out of the car and into his arms.

"I didn't have a key to get inside," Luke said.

Jamie laughed. "Oh my God, it is so good to see you. I've been worried to death."

He shrugged. "It wasn't so bad. I played video games the whole time."

Jamie resisted the urge to kick him. "Don't tell Poe," she warned. "I'm not sure he would take it as well as me."

Luke made a zipping gesture across his lips. "I won't say a word."

"Come on." Jamie ushered him toward the door. "There's a key under the mat."

"Who put a key under my welcome mat?" Luke frowned. "That's like the first place a burglar looks."

Jamie decided not to tell him that she'd put the key Abi had used under there in case she needed to come back. To her way of thinking, if Luke was missing, there was nothing else in the condo worth worrying about.

Inside, he looked around and groaned. "I need to water my plants."

"Pack your bag," Jamie told him. "I'll water your plants. We have a jet waiting for us."

They were going home. Together. For the first time in far too long.

Chicago
Tuesday, December 25

Christmas Day

Chapter Sixteen

Colby Residence,
7:00 p.m.

Victoria surveyed the buffet and the table in her dining room. Pride welled in her chest. She was so very grateful that her favorite caterer had been able to pull this off on such short notice.

Everything was perfect. The food, the desserts, the lovely drink venues. There was Wine Avenue in one corner, Champagne Falls—a fountain—in another and Everything Else Lane—with nonalcoholic choices—in yet another. The whole setup was so creative.

"It all looks lovely," Lucas said as he moved to her side.

She smiled up at him. "The decorations too." Lucas had been the one to oversee that part of the preparations. How he'd gotten holiday decorators on Christmas morning was a mystery. But then, Lucas was a man of many talents.

He'd never failed to accomplish a mission.

"I think we should share a private toast before the guests start to arrive," he suggested.

"Good idea."

They wandered to the champagne fountain and allowed the flowing bubbly to fill their glasses.

"To family," Lucas said as he tapped his glass against hers.

"Family," Victoria echoed. She closed her eyes and drank deeply. She was so very thankful that her family was home.

Jamie and Luke had arrived just before midnight last night. Victoria and Lucas had been up until two this morning just looking at those beautiful kids and pinching themselves. And listening to the story of all that happened in Nashville. The best part was that their grandchildren were safe, and they were home.

Jim and Tasha had arrived home this afternoon. The kids had gone to have some private time with them. Jim said they planned to tell them about the cancer and how fortunate they were that the treatment appeared to be doing its job. If all continued on this course, by spring Tasha would be cancer free.

It was all they could have hoped for.

"I think Poe is a very nice young man," Lucas said, drawing Victoria from her deep thoughts.

She smiled. "He is, and I'm quite certain he's madly in love with our Jamie."

"Well, of course he is," Lucas boasted. "She's brilliant, beautiful and…he doesn't deserve her."

Laughter bubbled from Victoria's throat. "You would say the same thing about anyone who showed an interest in her."

"I would. And I would be correct in my deduction."

Victoria nodded. "You would."

"She and I talked for a bit this morning," Lucas said before drinking more of his champagne.

"Really?" Victoria had seen the two of them having another cup of coffee after everyone else had left the kitchen this morning. "What did you talk about?"

"I asked her to come to work for the agency."

Victoria's heart skipped a beat. So many times she had wanted to ask Jamie that question, but she'd always satisfied her desperate hopes with simply letting Jamie know that she was welcome at the agency if she ever wanted to be there. Not once had Victoria come right out and asked.

"How did she react?"

Lucas inclined his head and considered the question for a moment. "She seemed surprised but not offended in any way. She asked me if the suggestion was only coming on the heels of the fright we had with Luke's kidnapping."

"What did you tell her?" Victoria couldn't wait to hear this.

"I told her that of course any and all things of that nature impacts our feelings, but this latest event wasn't the reason I asked."

Victoria's eyebrows went up. "I'm sure she was surprised by that claim."

Lucas shrugged one shoulder. "Perhaps, but it was true. I asked because I think we need her. The agency needs her. I've stayed on top of what she's doing for IOA. Like all these suitors, they don't deserve our granddaughter. She belongs at the Colby Agency."

Victoria struggled not to allow the sting in her eyes to become evident. "She is the one who should fill my shoes one day." Her voice wobbled a little, but it was the best she could do.

"Just a few weeks ago," Lucas went on, "Jim said the same thing."

Victoria felt taken aback by the news. "I wasn't suggesting Jim shouldn't run this agency. He has every right."

"He is aware of how you feel. You've asked him to do this before, but he always defers to your choices regarding agency matters."

This was true. She'd tried to retire, to turn the reins over to Jim, but he'd always come up with a reason that she should return.

"Do you think he feels as if I don't trust him or that anyone here doesn't trust his ability?" The notion twisted inside her like barbed wire. She loved her son. She wanted him to have what she and his father and Lucas had built. Jamie should be working with him and one day she absolutely should step into Victoria's shoes. But first, Jim would have his time.

"I think he doesn't trust himself to sit at the top. He loves this agency, and he loves being a part of it, but he does not want to be *the one*."

Victoria nodded. "I see. I'm sorry I didn't realize how he felt."

Lucas touched her cheek with a fingertip. "Jim doesn't make that easy."

This was true. She moistened her lips and asked, "What did Jamie say?"

"She wanted to think about it for a bit, but she promised to give us an answer soon."

At least it wasn't an immediate no. Victoria finished off her champagne. "That's all we can ask for."

"Indeed," Lucas agreed.

The doorbell rang and they put their glasses on a nearby tray and hurried to answer. Forget Paris. There was nothing like family and friends at Christmas.

Ian and Nicole were the first to arrive. In the next half hour, everyone from the agency who was available had arrived. It was a houseful for sure.

Victoria was so very thankful to see Tasha and Jim. Luke arrived with his parents, looking very handsome in a white suit, shirt and tie. Before she could grab Luke in a hug, he kissed her on the cheek.

"You look ravishing, Grandmother."

Victoria grinned. "Thank you, Luke. You look pretty amazing yourself." She hugged him and he kissed her temple and whispered, "I love you." She peered up at him. "Love you too." Then he hurried off to say hello to Lucas.

"Luke is right. You look great." Jim hugged her. "Merry Christmas, Mom."

Victoria hugged him fiercely. How she loved this man. "Merry Christmas to you and Tasha." She drew back, reached for her daughter-in-law and hugged her a bit more gently. "You two look incredible." How very strong this woman was. Victoria was so proud that she was the mother of her grandchildren.

"Thank you, Victoria." Tasha smiled. "And thank you for having this beautiful party."

Victoria barely restrained her tears, but she refused to cry considering all the blessings they had received in the past forty-eight hours. Lucas rescued her by coming for hugs of his own.

Lastly, Jamie and Kenny arrived. Victoria lost her breath when she saw the two of them. Jamie wore a pale blue sheath, and she looked stunning. She and her mother were nearly the same size and Victoria suspected the dress was Tasha's. Kenny looked quite dapper himself in a black formfitting suit, crisp white shirt and black tie. As a couple they were quite spectacular. The perfect power couple with their whole futures ahead of them. She hoped their relationship worked out.

The food tasted as wonderful as it looked. Lucas had set the Christmas music to a soft whisper and the smiles and laughter that filled their home was the perfect finishing touch. This Christmas was all that Victoria could ask for.

"Grandmother."

Victoria looked around to find Jamie standing beside her. To her gorgeous granddaughter she said, "I hope you're enjoying yourself."

Jamie smiled, the expression so big and beautiful it filled Victoria's heart with renewed pride. "I'm having a wonderful time." She hesitated a moment, then continued, "I spent some time this afternoon talking with Dad and then with Poe."

Victoria was afraid to breathe. Of all the things she had faced in her life, this might very well be one of the scariest.

"I've decided to put in my resignation at IOA and come to work with you and Grandpa."

As much as Victoria wanted to shout and jump for joy, she held it back and remained cool and calm. "That is wonderful to hear. And you're certain about this?"

Jamie laughed. "I am certain. I've been thinking about it for a long time. I'd like to be closer to my family. Running around all over the world has lost a bit of its mystique."

"If you change your mind…" Victoria offered.

"I will not," Jamie said resolutely. She looked across the room to Kenny. "You should know that Poe is coming as well, but I'll let him tell you."

Victoria beamed. "I am so pleased. I'm certain your father and mother are pleased as well."

Jamie's eyes turned a little watery then. "They're very happy about it."

Victoria hugged her granddaughter. "Merry Christmas, sweetheart."

Jamie drew back. "Merry Christmas to you, Grandmother."

"I hope I'm not too late."

The deep male voice with just a hint of a British accent drew everyone's attention to the man who'd entered the room.

"Abi," Jamie said. "I thought you couldn't come."

Looking very handsome in a black suit, shirt and tie, Abi crossed the room and pressed his cheek to Jamie's. "I rearranged a few things." He looked to Victoria then. "How often does one get invited to a Colby Agency party?" He gave Victoria the same treatment. "Thank you for inviting me."

Victoria gave him a nod. "Glad you could make it."

"Well, just look who the cat dragged in." Kenny appeared next to Jamie. He thrust out a hand. "Merry Christmas, Amar."

He shook the offered hand. "Merry Christmas, Poe."

Victoria decided that maybe this party had needed a little jolt of excitement and intrigue.

It was the perfect Colby Agency Christmas, as well as a celebration of the next generation.

* * * * *

*Don't miss the next installment of
the Colby Agency: The Next Generation
coming soon from Debra Webb
and Harlequin Intrigue!*

Here's a sneak peek of Alibi for Murder
available wherever books are sold.

Woodstock, Illinois
Friday, June 6
Foster Residence,
5:30 p.m.

"I hope you'll complete the survey when you receive it. We at GenCrop are always here for you, 24/7."

Allie Foster ended her final call for the day—for the next ten days actually—and removed the wireless headset. She exhaled a big breath, stood from her desk and stretched. There was something about Fridays even when she didn't have plans for the weekend or for her first vacation in years.

"Woo-hoo," she grumbled as she placed the headset on her desk. She shut off the desk lamp and walked out of her office. She was taking a vacation and going *nowhere*.

How exciting was that?

She would do yard work and maybe finally paint her bedroom. A really old-fashioned getaway from work. Wasn't she the globe-trotter?

Admittedly, Allie had always been a little on the old-fashioned side. It came from being raised by much older parents, she supposed. Technically, they were her grandparents. Her parents had died in a car accident when she was a toddler. She had only the faintest memories of them.

Allie banished the idea and focused on mentally shrugging off the workweek and the stress that often went with providing patient services. Answering calls all day might not sound like a tough job, but these were questions from patients who were, for the most part, terminally ill. Either they or a family member had questions about their medications or their appointments or just what they should do next. GenCorp was a huge medical operation. The services provided extended across the country and involved cutting-edge—sometimes experimental—pharmaceuticals, procedures and end-of-life patient care. Ultimately, there were always questions and it was her job to answer them or to find those answers.

What she needed now was to relax with her evening glass of wine and chocolate bar.

"Better than sex."

Probably not true, but it had been so long since she'd had sex that she wasn't entirely sure. But to believe this was the case made the idea of no prospects far more palatable and much less depressing.

No one's fault but your own, Al.

She wandered into the kitchen. One cupboard was dedicated to her favorite bottles of red. The drawer beneath the counter in that same spot held her chocolate stash. She was a simple girl. Many years from now, hopefully, when she was found dead and no doubt alone in the house, no one would think less of her for having plenty of wine and chocolate on hand.

Laughing at herself, she removed the cork from the bottle and poured a hefty serving. Wine and chocolate in hand, she retreated to the living room. The old box-style television still stood in the corner of the room. It was the perfect size for her aquarium. As she passed, she checked the automatic feeder to ensure it held an adequate amount.

"Hello, Nemo and friends." She tapped the glass and smiled as they darted around.

She frowned at the collection of dust on the dinosaur of a television. This was something else she needed to do on her vacation—dust, not replace the set. She hadn't watched it in years even before it died. The news was far too depressing, and the entertainment industry had stopped making decent movies ages ago.

She picked up her book from the side table and opened to the next chapter. Books never let her down.

Who needed television when they had books?

The buzz of the doorbell made her jump. For a moment she felt confident she must have imagined it. She had no deliveries scheduled. No one ever came to her door, not even neighbor's children selling cookies or other fundraising activities.

The buzzing sound came again and there was no denying it.

Someone was at her door.

Allie placed her glass and her book on the side table and stood. She wandered first to the front living room window and peeked out. A four-door sedan was parked in the drive. Dark in color, blue or black. No markings that suggested it was some sort of salesperson or business vehicle.

Since she couldn't see who had stepped up onto her porch from this window, she moved to the entry hall and had a look through the security viewer on the front door. One man, one woman. Both wore business suits. Both displayed serious facial expressions. Not the typical-looking salespeople. More like police officers or investigators of some sort.

Could be trouble in the neighborhood. A missing child.

Allie took a breath. She really disliked unannounced visits, but she certainly did not want to hinder the search for a criminal or a missing person. "Can I help you?" she asked through the door. It sounded better than "are you lost" as an opening.

The man withdrew a small leather case from an interior jacket pocket and opened it for Allie to see through the viewer. The credentials inside identified him as FBI special agent Elon Fraser. The photo matched his face, though he'd put on a few pounds since it was taken.

Why on earth would the FBI be calling on her?

"Would you state your business, please?" A reasonable request, in her opinion.

The female spoke up this time while simultaneously flashing her own credentials in front of the viewer. "We are here to speak with Allison Foster," Special Agent Uma Potter explained with visible impatience.

Allie opened the door and surveyed the two. "I'm Allison Foster."

Agent Potter gave her a steady perusal as well. "May we come in?"

"Of course." Allie stepped back and opened the door wider. The two crossed the threshold and waited while she closed and locked it.

"What are you here to talk about?" Allie asked, looking from one to the other. She had thought Fraser was lead. He was older and had knocked on the door, but maybe she'd been wrong.

"This may take some time," Potter suggested.

Allie nodded. "Follow me." She led the way to the living room, cringed at the sight of her half-finished glass of wine and chocolate bar on the table next to her favorite chair. "Have a seat." She gestured to the sofa.

Fraser waited for his colleague and then Allie to sit before doing the same.

Fraser began, "Ms. Foster, do you live here alone?"

Not exactly the sort of a question a woman who did live alone liked to answer when asked by a stranger, but the man was FBI, it seemed.

"Yes."

"Are there any weapons in the house?" he asked.

"Only my grandfather's BB rifle."

"Your grandmother left you this place?" This from Potter.

Allie nodded slowly. "She did." A frown worked its way across her forehead. "What's this about?" Why would the FBI want to know how she'd come into possession of her property?

She wondered if someone was trying to steal her property—she'd heard of this on one of the podcasts she occasionally tuned into. The house was the one thing of real value she owned. Worry needled her.

Potter pulled out her cell phone and tapped the screen. "You're thirty-two years old. Born to Alice and Jerry Foster, who died in an automobile accident when you were four." She glanced up at Allie when she said this as if to gauge her reaction.

"That's correct."

"Your mother's parents, Virginia and Gordon Holt, raised you. You graduated high school right here in Woodstock and went on to the nursing program at McHenry."

Now Allie was just annoyed. She straightened and held up her hands to stop her. "I'm not answering any more questions until you tell me what this is about."

Technically they weren't even questions, just recitations of the facts about her life to which she automatically agreed.

"You're employed by GenCorp," Fraser went on, taking the lead now that Allie had shown her irritation at Potter. "You started with them from their inception, ten years ago."

"Again," Allie said, "I will know what this is about before we continue the conversation."

"Ms. Foster," Potter resumed, "there was an incident at the hospital where you worked, which precipitated your leaving the hands-on side of the nursing field and moving to what you do now."

The memory of a patient dying in her arms caused Allie to flinch. She was not going back there. She stood. "I think we're done here."

There was absolutely no reason to talk about that tragedy. Allie had been investigated by the hospital, the nursing board and the local police. She had been cleared of wrongdoing. It was the doctor in charge of the case who'd made the mistake—Allie had only tried to save the poor woman and, sadly, all her efforts had failed.

"Please, bear with us, Ms. Foster," Fraser said, easing forward a bit, but not troubling himself to stand.

With visible reluctance, Allie settled into her chair once more. She barely resisted the urge to gulp down the rest of the wine in her glass. Not exactly the sort of move to make with two federal agents staring her down and going over her life history.

"One week ago," Fraser explained, "there was an incident at the hospital where you once worked. A patient was murdered in his room."

Allie drew back and sank deeper into her chair. "I'm sorry to hear that." She allowed a beat to pass. "But what does that have to do with me?"

"Did you see anything about it on the news?" Potter asked.

Finally, an actual question to answer. "I'm afraid not. I never watch the news." She shrugged. "I see the occasional headline pop up when I'm at the computer checking my e-mail, but I rarely follow the link or read whatever commentary accompanies it. I have a weather radio that keeps me informed of the weather, but that's about it really."

The two agents exchanged a glance.

"Can you tell us where you were on Friday, one week ago, from about five in the evening until midnight?"

Allie felt taken aback at the question. "Seriously?"

The way the two looked at her confirmed they were indeed serious.

She shrugged. "Okay. Let me confirm with my phone." She pulled up her calendar app. "I never do anything unless my phone tells me to." She laughed or attempted to laugh. The sound came out a little brittle. The agents watching her said nothing. Certainly didn't laugh. "Okay, here we go. That would have been May thirtieth and I worked from eight until five, then I had dinner and a shower and started a new book."

When the agents continued staring at her without uttering a word, she looked from one to the other. "*The Great Gatsby.* I've read it, like, five times, but I sometimes read it again when I haven't decided on something new."

"We've looked into your lifestyle," Fraser said.

A painful laugh burst out of her before Allie could stop it. Were they joking? "My lifestyle?"

"You don't leave the house often," he explained. "You order most everything online and have it shipped or delivered."

This time Allie's laugh was more sarcastic. "Since the

pandemic, lots of people use online ordering and home delivery. And when you work from home, you don't go out as often." What was the big deal with her shopping habits?

"Can you tell me the last time you left the house?" Potter inquired.

Allie drew in a deep breath and worked hard to tamp down the irritation that continued to rise. "I don't know. Maybe last month? I think my semiannual dental cleaning was last month. Maybe the fifth. I could check my calendar if you need an exact date."

"With Dr. Rice right here in Woodstock," Potter said.

Okay. Allie braced herself. It was one thing for these two to know her background, but to have been looking into her schedule and her comings and goings? Something was very wrong here.

Before she could say as much, Fraser spoke again. "Ms. Foster, we're here because the victim was part of an ongoing case the Bureau is deeply involved in."

Allie shook her head. "I don't see how my having worked an entire decade ago at the hospital involved has anything to do with your current case."

Again, the two exchanged one of those suspicious glances.

"Just get to the point please." She'd had more than enough of this game.

Potter tapped the screen of her cell again, then stood and moved to where Allie sat. "This might give you some clarification."

The screen was open to a video. A woman with brown hair dressed in scrubs paused at room 251. Allie frowned. The woman started into the room but paused long enough to glance first one way and then the other along the corridor, giving the camera a full-on shot of her face.

Allie zoomed in on the image and studied the face.

Hers.

The woman going into the room was *her.*

Puzzled, she stared up at Potter. "Why would you have this video? It has to be from at least ten years ago." Allie stared at the frozen image again. Her dark brown hair was in a ponytail, the way she'd always worn it—still did. She wore the required blue scrubs.

"This video," Potter explained, "is from one week ago. That room is where the patient was murdered."

"No. No. No." Allie snatched the phone from the agent's hand and watched the video again. "That's me rightly enough. But that was not a week ago." She paused the video and tried to zoom in much closer on her face, but it was too blurry to determine if the couple of crow's feet she had developed recently were absent—which to her way of thinking would be proof of when this video was done.

She shook her head, then passed the phone back to its owner. "I have no idea why you or anyone else would believe that video is only one week old. I haven't been in that hospital since—"

"Your grandmother died at the beginning of the pandemic," Fraser offered.

Allie blinked. "That's correct." She watched as Potter resumed her seat next to her colleague. "If you know this, then why are you suggesting that video is only a week old?"

"Because it is," Potter stated with complete certainty. "Every second of security footage from that hospital has been scrutinized repeatedly. The clip you watched is the one that occurred outside the victim's room just before he was murdered last Friday. There's another that shows you coming into the hospital that day, but nothing showing you leave."

This was wrong. Allie shook her head. "What you're suggesting is impossible."

Fraser moved his head slowly from side to side. "I wish it were."

No. This absolutely had to be some sort of mistake. "But you know I haven't been in that hospital for years." Worry started to climb up Allie's spine. They were serious. *This* was serious.

"The victim was Thomas Madison."

Allie rolled the name around in her head. "I don't know any Thomas Madison."

This was completely insane. She focused on slowing her breathing. The way her heart pounded, she was headed for a panic attack. She did not want to go there in front of these two.

"You may have seen him before." Fraser turned his cell toward her. The image displayed there was of a man who appeared to be in his late sixties to early seventies. Gray thinning hair. Light colored eyes. Saggy jowls.

"He doesn't look familiar."

"He worked with your father…before his untimely death."

Allie hesitated. "My father was a research technician at Ledwell…"

At the time—nearly thirty years ago—Ledwell had been the leading-edge AI research facility. Still was. Her father hadn't been a doctor or a scientist, just a tech, but he had been very good at his work. Her grandparents had told Allie stories about how good he was. Most of those in charge at Ledwell had believed him to be far better than any of their academically trained scientists.

"Did you know," Fraser said, "there was an investigation into your parents' accident?"

"I can't say that I knew it growing up but, looking back, I'm sure that would have been the case. Aren't all accidents, particularly those involving deaths, investigated?"

"Usually, yes," Fraser admitted. "But there was more to your parents' accident. There was some question about whether it was an accident."

The wallop that slammed into her chest was Allie's own heart. She gasped and fought to calm herself. "Do you have any evidence of what you're telling me?"

Fraser said, "I don't have all the details, but suffice to say there were questions. None of which were answered, in my opinion. At any rate, the case was closed and that was the end of it."

Allie got up. She had to move. She started to pace and didn't care what her guests thought. Why wouldn't her grandparents have told her this? "What does my parents' accident have to do with this Mr. Madison and his murder?"

"We don't know," Potter admitted. "That's what we'd like to find out. Which is why we're here."

Allie paused and aimed a what-the-heck expression at her. "How would I know? I was four years old when they died."

"Right," Potter agreed. "We're hoping your grandparents left notes, letters or some sort of information about the investigation back then that will give us some insight. The local law enforcement office suffered a fire in the storage area where old case files were kept, so there's nothing on the investigation."

Allie digested this information. "If my grandparents kept anything related to the accident, I am unaware of it." They never talked about the accident. Plenty was said about her parents, of course. In part, to ensure Allie knew how much they had loved her and to help her remember them, but not about that awful day other than exactly that—what an awful day it was.

"We assumed as much," Fraser said. "We hoped you might allow us to have a look around the house—unless of course you've purged any and all old papers and files."

"No. I would never do that. This was their home. Their papers and other things are right where they left them." It was a big old rambling house. No need to purge. Not that she would have anyway.

"Then you won't mind if we look for anything useful on finding the truth about what happened to your parents?" This from Potter.

Yes was on the tip of Allie's tongue, but then logic kicked in. "You came here to question me about a murder." She looked to Fraser. "You have a video—or two—that seem to show me entering the hospital and then the room of the victim on the day of the murder and, I'm assuming, around the time of his death. But then you segued into my parents' accident."

"Because we feel the two are related," Fraser insisted.

"Twenty-eight years apart," she countered.

"Yes," Fraser insisted.

"So you're looking for any thoughts, notes, letters, et cetera my grandparents may have kept related to the accident. You're not here to find evidence that would somehow prove your theory about me going into that hospital room and murdering a patient." This was not a question, she already knew the answer.

"Oh no," Fraser said with a flippant expression and a wave of his upright palms. "We're certainly not looking to railroad anyone. We're here to find the truth."

"So your search warrant will be very specific about what you're looking for," Allie suggested.

"If one is required," Fraser said. "I don't see any need to make it that sort of formal search. Agent Potter and I could just have a quick, casual look around as long as you're agreeable."

Allie almost laughed out loud. These two clearly thought she was a naive shut-in. Obviously, they also thought she was a murderer.

Bottom line, she had no idea whatsoever if her parents' accident was anything other than an accident. She also had no clue as to whether their accident was related to this murder at the hospital. And she certainly did not know the victim.

But what she did know was a fishing expedition when she saw one.

Allie paused in her pacing. "Well, thank you for stopping by and giving me so much to consider." She gestured toward the entry hall. "But I believe we're quite finished here."

"You're refusing to cooperate with our investigation," Potter suggested.

Allie smiled at the less than subtle pressure technique. "No. I'm just choosing to take advantage of my legal right to say no. Not without a warrant. Now, if you'll excuse me, I have a glass of wine and a chocolate bar to finish."

With another of those shared looks, the two federal agents rose from the sofa and walked to the front door. Once they were gone, Allie secured the door, then went to a window to watch them drive away.

She wondered how long it would be before they were back with a warrant and a team of fellow agents to prowl through her belongings.

There really wasn't a reason she could think of that she should care. But the fact that they had a video showing her in the hospital, supposedly one week ago, entering the room of a man who was murdered, was reason enough to take a moment to think this through. As much as she would love to believe it was just some sort of mistake—a woman who looked like her—this was not the case.

This was something very, very wrong.

She had no family attorney. She had no friends who were in the legal profession.

In truth she had lost touch with anyone she had considered a friend years ago. Not due to any falling outs or disagreements. Just because she wasn't much of a socializer, and it had simply been easier to focus on work and taking care of her grandmother and then the pandemic had come along.

Life changed.

She leaned against the locked door and racked her brain for anyone who might be able to advise her. Someone she could trust.

Wait.

Steve Durham.

He'd joined the police department in Chicago when he graduated high school. She remembered him well. He was a year older, but she'd had a serious crush on him. The last she'd heard, he had gone on to law school and eventually landed at a prestigious firm in Chicago. What was the name of it?

Oh yeah. *The Colby Agency.*

Alibi for Murder *will be published August 2025.*
Pick up a copy wherever Harlequin Books are sold.

HARLEQUIN
Reader Service

Enjoyed your book?

Try the perfect subscription for Romance readers and get more great books like this delivered right to your door.

See why over 10+ million readers have tried Harlequin Reader Service.

Start with a Free Welcome Collection with free books and a gift—valued over $20.

Choose any series in print or ebook. See website for details and order today:

TryReaderService.com/subscriptions